Badger on the Barge
and Other Stories

Janni Howker

BADGER
ON THE
BARGE
and Other Stories

Greenwillow Books
New York

Library of Congress Cataloging in Publication Data

Howker, Janni.   Badger on the barge, and other stories.
Contents: Badger on the barge—Reicker—The egg-man—[etc.]
1. Short stories, English. [1. England—Fiction.   2. Short Stories] I. Title.
PZ7.H845Bad   1984   [Fic]   84-10293   ISBN 0-688-04215-5

Contents

Badger on the Barge

For Carole

OCTOBER smelled of bonfires, even in Alfred Street. Down by the canal the yellow leaves of the big conker trees flickered and rustled like burning newspapers. In the still canal water black leaves floated on Helen's reflection.

"Come,ye thankful people, come,
Raise the song of harvest home.
All is safely gathered in
'Ere the winter storms begin..." she sang softly. Across the canal she could see King Alfred's Grammar School, high and holy on its hill above the empty cricket-field. Peter didn't go there any more.

At last Helen took the list out of her basket. All the names were crossed off except one. 'Miss Brady. The Barge. The Canal.' Underneath, Mrs Phillips, her teacher, had written: *Boat moored on the canal just past the bridge.* In her basket was the last box of fruit from their school harvest festival which she had to deliver to old age pensioners. So far Helen had not enjoyed knocking on the old people's doors, drinking cups of sweet tea and looking at photographs of smug grandchildren who never came to call.

Miss Brady would be the seventh, and the last.

She stood looking at the towers of the Grammar School for a few seconds more, then she turned and walked along the muddy towpath. Peter didn't go there any more. And, this morning, Dad had burnt his cricket bat on that terrible bonfire, while Mum had stood at the back door, silently watching. Mum had looked as worn and grey as a length of old string.

3

"Come,ye thankful people, come,
    Raise the song of harvest home..." she sang again, be-
cause the tune was in her head, and it stopped her thinking
about Peter. She stepped over a puddle then went under the
arch of the stone bridge. She did not hurry. She did not want
to hear about another old person's arthritis, nor did she want
to go home yet. The bonfire was still burning on the
allotment behind their house.

October smelled of bonfires, but after today bonfires
would never smell the same again. Like everything else since
April, wood smoke had become sad.

The barge was moored by the towpath. Although she
quite often came by the canal on her way home from school,
she had never seen it there before. Or perhaps it was just that
she had not come by the canal for a long time. Frowning, she
tried to remember.

The boat was long and low, and brightly painted. The hull
was black, with green rubbing strakes and a red gunnel. The
panels on the cabin sides were painted with roses – four
flowers making a diamond shape. A striped green and red
pole stuck out of the end. From a distance it looked like a
picture in a book, but close to, Helen saw that some of the
paint was peeling, and there was a heap of dirty straw on the
small semi-circular poop-deck.

A plank led from the towpath to the deck, but Helen was
not sure what to do. She could see the little cabin door with
roses painted on it, but she was not sure she should go
aboard. Crouching, she tried to see in through the windows,
but the curtains were drawn.

Everything was quiet on the black water of the canal. The
sun hung like a red balloon in the branches of the horse-
chestnut tree. Only a swan came sailing, leaving a wake of
ripples, from under the bridge. It was white on the water, all
alone.

"Here, Cobbler! Here, cob, cob, cob... Here, Cobbler!"
called a voice from the barge. "There's a good fellow.
There's a grand lad." It was an old voice. The barge rocked
gently as someone moved inside.

Helen stepped back. A thin yellow arm and hand appeared through a window on the far side of the boat. The swan arched its neck. A few scraps of bread floated towards him and he clicked at them with his yellow beak. Wagging his white tail feathers, he glided out of sight behind the barge.

The hand reappeared, poking through the window, and tossed some more bread. "There's a grand old lad who can't sing for his supper. There's my old faithful Cobbler..." said the voice.

Helen wished she had some bread to throw for the swan, but her basket contained only the box of apples and oranges. Nothing that swans liked, she thought. Anyway, at least she had a reason to go on board. She walked up the gang-plank. "Hello?"

No one answered. Then the barge lurched. The cabin doors were pushed open a crack.

"Who is it? What do you want?" The voice did not sound friendly.

"I'm Helen Fisher, from Heighton School. I've brought you a basket from our harvest festival," said Helen, for the seventh time today.

"Beg your pardon?" said the old voice. The cabin door opened a bit wider, and an eye looked at her from the dark crack.

"I'm Helen Fisher. This is for you, from our harvest festival." She took the box of fruit from her basket.

The swan slid away nervously. Autumn leaves rippled against the canal bank.

"Is it now? Then I expect you'll have to come in. Quickly, girl!" The door was pushed open. Helen climbed down the three steps of the companionway and found herself standing before Miss Brady.

The old woman's hair was grey and white in streaks, tied back in a bun. Her face was as thin and brown as cardboard, with deep lines round her nose and mouth. One leg was stretched stiffly in a bandage, her heel resting on a coil of rope. She was wearing a long brown skirt and a tweed jacket with leather patches on the elbows. She still held a slice of bread in her hand.

"Well, close the door."

Helen pulled it shut with a bang.

"Shhh!" hissed Miss Brady. "Now, talk quietly."

Mrs Phillips had told Helen to speak up when she called on old age pensioners, but she did not dare disobey the fierce old woman.

"I'm Helen Fisher," she whispered.

"Yes, yes, I heard," snapped Miss Brady. "Now what's this?"

Inside, the barge was long and thin and low, but surprisingly roomy. There were shelves, a small sink and cooker, bare boards, a black stove, and pieces of rope tied in incredible knots hanging on the cabin walls. A cushion lay on the floor, with a hole torn in it and all its stuffing falling out.

"From our harvest festival," Helen whispered. She looked at the old woman who was watching her suspiciously. There was a strange smell in the boat, strong and sour. On the floor were two saucers. One was full of milk and the other was full of... Helen looked again. It was full of raw liver and worms. Some of the worms wriggled.

"This is for me, is it? Well, well," said the old woman. "A booby prize for hurting my leg, I suppose." She glanced at the box of fruit, but she did not seem pleased. "Wonder which nosey do-gooder told them about me? Put it on the sink, out of harm's way."

Surprised, Helen did as she was asked. All the other old people had been delighted – or at least that's what they said. The sink and draining-board were quite small, like toys. Through a sliding door she could see a big heap of hay and leaves under a bunk. The cushion which made the seat of the bunk looked as if it had been slashed with a knife, and all the foam was bursting out. The smell was stronger, almost a stink.

Tree shadows flickered through the cabin, reflected up from the water.

"Might as well make yourself useful, girl, seeing as you're here. Put the kettle on, will you? There's matches on the shelf."

Helen frowned. The old woman did not say please or thank you. She just gave orders like a blooming soldier!

"Here, Cobbler. Come on, you old devil." Miss Brady threw some more bread through the window. When she talked to the swan her voice was gentler than when she talked to Helen.

"Is that his name, then?" Helen asked, as she lit the gas and put the kettle on. She was trying to be friendly. She liked being in the boat, but she was not at all sure about Miss Brady.

"What?"

"Cobbler. Is that his name?"

"Lord, no!" said Miss Brady, with a sharp unfriendly laugh. "Swans don't have names! They're not like dogs, you know. It's just a noise he comes to. I only call cobbler because its like cob. Cobs are male swans, you see?"

"Oh," said Helen. She felt a bit flustered, as if she had asked a stupid question in class.

"And you're Helen, eh?" Miss Brady gave her a long look. "Pleased to meet you, I suppose." She held out her hand.

"How do you do?" Helen said politely, shaking hands. She had never shaken hands with a woman before. It seemed odd.

"Could be better. Oh Lord!" Miss Brady exclaimed, staring at the floor by Helen's feet. "Put that worm back on the saucer, will you?"

"Yack!" Helen stepped away from it. It was a big purple worm slithering by her shoe.

"It won't bite you, girl!"

"I don't like worms," Helen said, pulling a face.

"Well, pick it up with that bit of newspaper then." Miss Brady glared at her and shook her head. Her look made Helen feel silly.

Quickly, she snatched up the worm and dropped it back on the saucer with the rest. Some of them were swimming in the blood from the raw liver. It made her feel a bit sick.

"You see," crowed the old woman. "It didn't bite."

"It felt horrible and slimy though." Helen wiped her

fingers down her jeans. "What do you want with worms?"

But Miss Brady only gave her a quick smile and said, "Kettle's boiling. Teapot's on the shelf. Takes two spoons. Then you'd better be off."

Helen decided she did not like this old woman one little bit. She was bossy, and, somehow, she made Helen feel misjudged. Just because she had not wanted to pick up the worm, Miss Brady had decided she was soft and silly – which wasn't fair.

Miss Brady's face looked hard as a table leg, except for her cheek-bones which stuck out a little and were pale. Sometimes she caught her breath when she moved, as if her ankle hurt badly.

She could open tins with that blooming sharp nose! thought Helen crossly as she spooned the tea into the pot.

"Milk's in the cupboard. Mug's on the draining-board."

There was only one mug. Obviously, she was not going to invite Helen to stay for a cup. Helen felt annoyed. After all, she had brought her a present from school.

"Thank you," said Miss Brady, for the first time, as Helen handed her the mug. "Ah, that's the stuff." She sipped the tea.

"I suppose I'd better be going then," said Helen, still half expecting to be offered some tea or a toffee.

"Right-ho!"

Helen scrambled back out onto the deck, stopped, and looked back at the old woman, puzzled. She'd never met anyone like her. "Is there anything you want me to do, like? I mean with you having a gammy leg?"

Miss Brady peered at her over her mug of tea. "Well now. There is one thing, come to think of it."

Oh no, thought Helen. She did not really want to go shopping or fetching library books for a bossy old bag. She wished she hadn't opened her mouth. She had only asked out of politeness. "Yes?"

"Worms," said Miss Brady. "You could fetch me a bucket full of worms and soil."

"Worms?" Helen stared at her.

"Worms," said the old woman. "You know, those horrible slimy things that you don't like?"

"Oh. I suppose so. I'll try and bring some tomorrow."

"Promise, Helen Fisher?" Suddenly, Miss Brady's face looked much thinner and older.

"Alright. I promise," said Helen. "Tarra."

"Au-revoir!" called Miss Brady.

"God our maker does provide
  For our wants to be supplied . . ." Helen sang as she ran down the towpath towards home. Worms! she thought. Perhaps she eats them! and she swung her empty basket high into the air.

At home the silence made her head ache. Mum and Dad hardly talked any more. Some of the pictures were missing off the top of the piano – photographs of Peter in his blazer, of Peter kneeling in front of the school football team with his arms folded, of Peter astride his new motorbike with his crash helmet under his arm and a big daft grin on his face. That's how the police had found him – with his crash helmet under his arm, lying by the side of the road. Helen's pictures were still there, but no one looked at them anymore.

She still cried for Peter sometimes, but not the way Dad did. Dad had never cried on the outside, but inside he cried all the time. Peter had been everything to Dad. Peter had gone to grammar school. Peter was going to be an engineer. Peter was the spitting image of his dad, a chip off the old block, everyone said.

It was dark now. Helen could not sit there in silence with her mam any longer. Today was worse than usual, because of the bonfire.

"Where's me dad?" she asked at last.

"Still up on the allotment. I do wish he'd come in."

"Shall I fetch him, Mam?"

"You can try, love. Perhaps he'll come down with you."

Helen went out of the back door. Dad was silhouetted against the yellow flames and orange smoke. His black figure was hunched against the darkness among the knobbly silhouettes of brussel sprouts. He was leaning on a garden fork. He looked like an old man.

"Dad?" she went up into the allotment and stood by him.

"Hello, love." He straightened up. "Well, that's the lot. Everything."

"Good," said Helen. And she meant it. Perhaps now he'll take some notice of me, she thought. Then she felt guilty. She knew what Dad had been thinking all day as he stared into the bonfire. Why did we ever buy him that motorbike? If only . . . If only . . . He had said it over and over again, at first.

Dad had forgotten she was there. "Dad?"

"Sorry, love. Miles away."

"Can I dig up some worms from the allotment tomorrow?"

"If you like. What do you want with worms?"

"For an old woman that lives on the canal."

But he was hardly listening, she could see. He was staring at the pulsing embers where little red flames were licking up around a charred leather glove. The smell of burning leather came creeping through the smoke.

"Dad? Mam says to come in now."

"In a minute, tell her."

"But Dad," said Helen, quietly.

"I'll not be long."

But he was still standing there when Helen drew her bedroom curtains – alone, in the darkness, watching the wind blow sparks across the big harvest moon.

2

"YOU'RE NOT going to school dressed like that," said Dad at breakfast. She was wearing her jeans and wellingtons and an old red jumper.

"It isn't school today, Dad. It's Sunday. Anyway," she added, "I don't like school anymore."

"Why, love?" Mum was in her best dress. She had started going to church since Peter died, but Dad would not go, and she did not make Helen go with her either.

Helen shrugged. "Nobody is me real friend any more, since Peter got killed. I mean, they're very nice and that, but nobody 'ull be me proper friend." It was true. Sometimes when she cried, she cried because she was lonely. Even Ann Jackson, who had been her best friend in spring, would not come round for tea any more, because of the silence in the house. Helen had overheard her in the playground saying that she felt right sorry for that Helen Fisher, her dad's gone really morbid.

Neither Mum nor Dad said anything. It was a kind of rule that nobody said a word about Peter in front of Dad. She had just broken the rule, and they were pretending she hadn't. Sometimes the silence made Helen feel like shouting. Mum was sitting there, looking thin but smart. She was alright. She sometimes talked about Peter when Dad was out. But Dad was in his shirt-sleeves. He hadn't bothered to shave for the last few days. Sometimes he didn't even go into work any more.

It made Helen afraid.

She knew things about Peter that he did not know. She knew Peter had smoked and sworn when he was with his mates, and he had been with them when they smashed all the windows in the phone box. Once she had heard him call Dad 'a right soft touch' for buying him the bike. But Dad thought Peter was an angel. He did not know Peter had wanted to be a Hell's Angel.

Suddenly, Helen felt very glad she had met old Miss Brady. At least there was somewhere to go today, and something to do.

After breakfast, she followed Dad up onto the allotment. In the past, his had always been the neatest plot, but now it was as scruffy as the rest. He stood for a long time, staring at the black circle of cinders where the bonfire had been, then he began to turn the soil over with his spade. Black to brown at each big spadeful, until only brown was left, and all the ashes were under the earth.

As he dug, Helen picked up worms on a trowel and dropped them in a tin bucket.

11

"Eh, lass," said Dad. "You're worse than a blooming robin – hopping about after worms in your red jumper!"

"I've got twelve."

"Well, you'd find more if you turned over those flower pots," said Dad, leaning on his spade. "See? By the shed. And try the compost heap and all."

"Ta, Dad."

He watched her for a moment, as if he had not seen her for a very long time, then he started to dig again, but more slowly.

Soon she had half a bucket of worms and soil. It was so heavy she could only just carry it with two hands. "Bye!" she called.

"Tarra!" Dad waved back.

She struggled down Alfred Street with the heavy bucket, smiling to herself because Dad had waved, until the bucket bashed her on the knee and made her swear.

"Oh, it's you." Miss Brady pushed open the cabin door. It was not much of a welcome.

"I've brought your worms, like I promised. Are you alright?" Miss Brady's face was as yellow as sponge cake and there were black shadows under her cheekbones.

"Course I am!" snapped the old woman. "Now keep your voice down, will you?"

"Sorry," murmured Helen.

"It's Bad Bill," said Miss Brady. "Don't want to wake him. He's not in the best of tempers, bein' cooped up like this."

"Who's Bad Bill?"

"Bad Bill the Badger." Miss Brady pointed into the next cabin, where the dark lump of straw and hay was heaped under the bunk.

Helen stared at the straw. "A real badger, you mean?"

"Yes, yes. A real live kicking and biting badger." She smiled at Helen. It made her face look better. "And, thank the Lord, he's asleep."

"A badger, on a barge?" Helen could not believe it. She had never seen a real badger. "Is that what smells funny?"

"Same family as polecats, you know. They're all a bit smelly. Usually, he lives in a big pen down the canal, but I had to bring him with me when I hurt my ankle. Had to go to hospital, you see, for stitches. Couldn't just leave him. But it's no good, a badger on a boat, even if we are old friends."

Miss Brady had a dry, posh voice. She clipped the ends off words and addressed Helen as if she were a public meeting.

"Bad Bill," said Helen. "So badgers have names, even if swans don't."

Miss Brady scowled at her, then she burst out laughing. "Touché! You've nailed me there, Helen Fisher!"

Helen grinned. "Shall I put the kettle on – seeing as I'm here?" She wanted to stay. She wanted to see the badger.

"Good idea," said the old woman. "Could do with a cuppa – the old devil had me up all night. Gallivantin' and rampagin' round the cabin. Tryin' to dig his way out, you know. Poor old Bill," she added more gently. Her face went hard again. "There's another mug in the locker there – if you want to stay a mo."

"Great!" said Helen. She poured tea for them both. "Does he like worms, then? I can get you tons off me Dad's allotment if you want."

"Worms, dead chicks, meat, maize, he's partial to all sorts. But his favourite is honey. He'd eat it until he was as fat as butter if I let him." Then, just as she seemed friendly, Miss Brady's voice changed. "Quickly, girl! Get out of the door! Go on, hurry!"

She grabbed Helen by the arm, making her spill her tea, and thrust her towards the companion-way. She was surprisingly strong.

Startled, Helen climbed out onto the deck. The door closed to a tiny crack behind her. She heard a rustle and a thud like a heavy ball bouncing.

"Sorry," called Miss Brady. "Didn't mean to frighten you – it's just that he's a bad-tempered old devil at the moment. Might just bite, you know."

Helen breathed her relief. She'd thought Miss Brady had gone mad. "Can I look?" she whispered.

"Yes. But keep still."

Helen peered in through the crack. Beside her, the smell of damp earth rose from the bucket of worms she had left on the deck. For the first time ever, she saw a badger. The black and grey striped head poked through the door, and then came the fat rippling skirting-board of his body. Like a grey shadow, he moved out of the far cabin – then he was like a fat bear, bouncing along, thumping the planks, making a chickering snuffling whinny, like a tiny horse. His claws clicked and scratched on the wood. He lifted his striped snout towards the old woman, as if he was looking at her from out of his black nose, then he buried his face in the milk, and slurped and guzzled, noisy as a pig.

"Heck..." whispered Helen. "He's ace!"

"Come here, you silly old lump," said Miss Brady. The badger came bouncing up to her, like a grey rug being shaken. He reared on his hind legs and she rubbed his small round ears. "What are you doing up at this time of day?"

Helen half expected to hear him purr. He made a pleased snuffling noise and rushed back to his saucer of worms.

Clock-clock, chop, went his teeth on the clicking saucer. When the worms were all gone he shoved his nose under the saucer and flipped it over. Sniffing here and there, he ambled back to the far cabin and nosed his way back into the heap of straw. After a bit of shoving and snorting, he disappeared from view.

They were both silent a while longer. Then Miss Brady said, "Coast's clear. You can come back in."

"Would he really bite me?" He had looked very tame to Helen.

"Perhaps. Can't take chances. A wild badger wouldn't come near you, but that old devil might. Might think you're an unfriendly badger trespassing on his territory, you see."

Helen nodded. "I wish I had a badger for a pet."

"Oh, he's no pet," said Miss Brady, shaking her head. "He's a trial and a torment, bless him." She gazed at the upturned saucer, the lines deepening around her thin nose and mouth. She continued talking, quietly, while the sunlight on the water made rippling reflections on the cabin wall above her head. "I'm an obstinate old woman, Helen Fisher. Don't care for people – never have. Especially children. Can't bear brats." She glanced up, her thin lips pressed tightly together.

Helen smiled. "Don't you like me, even?" For a moment, she thought the old woman was joking with her, but when she saw the look on Miss Brady's face she knew she was not.

The old woman was not smiling at all. "Probably not. Can't see why I should change the habits of a life-time just for you, girl."

Helen did not know what to say. Miss Brady baffled her. She wished the badger would come out again. "You must like somebody . . . "

"I must, must I? Hmmmph!" the old woman snorted.

"Well, I hate being lonely," said Helen quietly.

"Do you?"

"Yes."

"Me. I like it. Not lonely, but being alone. Suits me. Shall I tell you something?"

Helen nodded.

"Hundreds of old people are lonely, and if you went to see them they'd think the sun shone out of your eyes. Funny, isn't it? Here I am, and the last thing I want is people. People fussing and changing things."

Helen felt she was being tested, or challenged. Miss Brady was watching her across the cabin.

"I won't change anything," she said.

"No," said Miss Brady. "No, I don't think you would." She smiled at Helen. "Thank you for bringing the worms."

"Anyway," Helen added. "You aren't alone – you've got Bad Bill and Cobbler."

Miss Brady shook her head. "Not for long."

From the heap of straw came a long piggy snore. Helen laughed. "He sounds just like me dad!"

"Oh Lord!" muttered the old woman, staring at her bandaged ankle. "I hate askin' for help."

15

Helen waited. Although the badger was still snoring, the boat seemed very quiet now.

"Got to go into hospital, you see. Bad Bill can't stay here."

For one wonderful moment, Helen thought Miss Brady was going to ask her to look after him. But Miss Brady didn't.

"Will you help me to the phone box, Helen? There's a chap at Wharmton Nature Reserve who'll take him."

"Take him away? For good?"

"Yes."

"But I could look after him! Honest!"

"No, you couldn't. He isn't like a cat or a dog, Helen. He's a big boar badger who wants a mate soon, and a sett, and who doesn't care for people any more than I do. I've done my best for him – found him drownin' in the canal in March. He was only small then – well, it's time for us to part company."

"But I'd feed him every day!" cried Helen. "I'd dig up worms and bring him honey."

But Miss Brady only shook her head and held out her mug of tea. "I think I could do with a drop of brandy in this, girl. There's a bottle in that cupboard."

Helen fetched it for her. "But won't you miss him?"

"Lord, yes! Oh, I'll miss him alright, the old vandal. Look what he's done to my cushions." She smiled sadly.

"If he was mine I'd keep him for ever and ever."

Miss Brady stared at her down her long beaky nose. She looked like a crow staring down from a tree. "When you're my age, Helen, there's no such thing as ever and ever. Besides, it'd be cruel to keep him. Come on, help me hop to the phone."

It was hard work getting Miss Brady to the phone box and back, even though it was not very far. Every time she put her foot down she said, "Oh damn! Oh Lord!" and, "The devil take it!" until Helen had to bite her lip to stop herself getting the giggles.

By the time they were back on board, Helen's shoulder ached with the weight of the old woman leaning on her.

16

Miss Brady dropped down onto the bunk and drank a mouthful of brandy straight from the bottle. She closed her eyes.

"Are they coming to take him, then?"

"Yes. Tomorrow. Bringin' a land-rover to collect him. It's for the best, you know. It's for the best." But Miss Brady did not open her eyes. She sat with her leg stuck out stiffly and the brandy bottle resting in her lap.

"Miss Brady?"

"Yes?"

"Can I bring me mam and dad to see him before he goes?"

Miss Brady took another swig from the bottle. "Well, I don't know . . ." she said. Then she banged the cork back into the bottle with the palm of her hand. "Oh, why the devil not!"

Helen laughed. "After tea?" She had never heard anyone swear like Miss Brady.

"Alright."

"Tarra!" Helen yelled as she ran down the gangplank, and the Town Hall clock chimed four through the clear golden air.

"Some other time," said Dad. "I'm busy this evening." He switched on the television, but Helen's mum went and turned it off. She stood stiffly, looking at Dad.

"Busy doing what? For Heaven's sake, John! Helen only wants to show us something! And when did you ever see a badger!"

Dad sat silently, his gaze fixed on the blank screen.

"You're never interested in what I do!" cried Helen. She had thought Dad would be pleased. His silence was like an iron door shut between them. "It's always Peter, Peter, Peter!" she yelled, as if she was banging on the door with her fists. "Sometimes I hate Peter!" She ran upstairs and slammed the bedroom door behind her. The tears were like hot insects crawling on her face.

From downstairs came the sound of Mum's voice, sharp as broken glass. She put her hands over her ears and stared out

17

of the window. The trees above the allotment looked as if they were on fire; then the sun went, and they were like burned sticks against the pale red sky.

"Helen?" her mam came in quietly. "Come on. Get your coat. Your dad's waiting."

"He doesn't want to go."

"Of course he does, really." Mum came and stood by the window.

"No, he doesn't. It's just that you've made him."

Mum sighed. "Perhaps, love. Perhaps. But I want to go."

"Mam. I didn't mean what I said about Peter."

Mum nodded. "I know, Helen. Come on."

Dad was waiting in the hallway. "Sorry, love," he said. But it was no good, thought Helen. She had wanted to show him the badger. Now it seemed all spoiled.

Together they walked through the October evening, down Alfred Street to the canal. The smell of wood smoke hung on the cold air, and a huge yellow moon was rising and trembling over the towers of the Grammar School. Another moon rippled on the black water of the canal.

"It's a long time since I came down here," said Dad, stopping. "We used to go fishing by that bridge when I was a lad. Me and young Mick Baker. Once caught a pike as long as me arm." He stood looking at the shapes of the school high on the dark hill. "Used to chuck stones across the canal at the Grammar School lads. Never thought a son of mine would go there..."

"Come on," said Mum, taking Helen's arm. "Where's this badger on the barge? Hey! It sounds like a song, our Helen,

Badger on the barge
Badger on the barge
Eee-i, me laddy-o
Badger on the barge!"

She was trying to stop Dad thinking about Peter. Helen squeezed her hand.

"There's the boat. Hush, Mam. You'll frighten him."

"Who? Your dad?" Mum laughed. "I never thought my singing was that bad!"

18

They stayed outside on the small deck, watching through the open door. A small calor gas lamp hissed on the cabin wall, yellow as the moonlight. Miss Brady said hello, then passed up the bottle of brandy and two mugs, to keep the cold out, but she didn't invite them in.

"Cheers!" said Dad.

"Bottoms up and the devil take the hindmost!" said Miss Brady, raising her mug.

Mum stared at her, then glanced at Helen. Helen pressed her hand over her mouth, to stop herself laughing at the look on her mam's face.

"There!" she whispered, tugging Mum's sleeve. Along the cabin floor came the badger, thumping and snuffling like a small pig under a rug.

"Well I never!" gasped Dad, who was kneeling beside her. "It really is a badger! Look at the stripes on his head."

"Told you!"

"Now then, you old rascal..." murmured Miss Brady, reaching down to scratch his broad back. Bad Bill lifted his striped mask and sniffed at the cabin door, alert and wary. Then he backed away, burying his snout between his front paws and humping his back. He stayed like that for a moment, then rolled over, grabbed the torn cushion and flung it down the cabin.

For nearly an hour they knelt in silence on the cold deck, watching the badger play in the gas-lit cabin, while Miss Brady told them a little about him. Mum and Dad both seemed a bit shy of Miss Brady, but she hardly looked at them.

Crouched between them, with Mum's handbag sticking in her ribs, Helen stole sips of Dad's brandy. The yellow moon sailed through the branches of the conker tree, a frosty mist curled on the water, and Bad Bill the badger snouted his way through the stuffing of the torn cushions for all the world as if it were a heap of autumn leaves.

"Well I never!" Dad kept saying as they walked home through the dark streets. "Well, there's a thing!"

"And what a funny old woman your Miss Brady is," said Mum when they got in.

"Aye, a right old trooper, that one." Dad took off his coat and hung it on the peg. "I think she was drunk as a lord!" He chuckled.

"Oh no," said Helen. "She's always like that."

"Well, we'll have to dig up some more worms for old Bill Brock tomorrow. He eats 'em like spaghetti."

"He won't be there tomorrow, Dad. That's why you had to come tonight. He's going to a nature reserve."

"Still," said Dad, smiling. "A badger, eh? Well, I never did!"

And until bed-time that night, the silence had gone from the house.

3

BY MORNING the silence had surged back, and Dad was quiet again. He wandered up onto the allotment after breakfast, and did not go to work. All through school that day Helen thought about the badger, hoping against hope that Miss Brady had kept him after all. Then she could take Dad to see him again.

As soon as school was over, she ran to the canal – just in case. When she got to the bridge she saw the ambulance parked on the towpath. Two men were carrying Miss Brady down the gang-plank. Cobbler stood on the far bank, preening his wide white wing.

"Miss Brady!" Helen ran up to them.

The old woman looked as light as a leaf as she sat on the cradle of the men's crossed arms. The men smiled at Helen.

"Has he gone?"

"Yes. Land-rover came at lunchtime. He was quiet as a lamb, Helen." Miss Brady's face looked thin and sad. "It is for the best, you know. Tonight he'll be ambling around in the moonlight under the trees, not stuck in a smelly old boat."

"And you'll be tucked up in a nice warm bed," said one of the men.

"Hmmmph!" Miss Brady snorted like a camel.

"I'll come and see you," Helen said. "And I'll look after the barge if you want."

"Then you'd better have a key." Miss Brady reached into the pocket of her tweed jacket. "Here."

The men carried her carefully into the back of the ambulance and closed the doors.

"Will she be alright?" Helen could just see Miss Brady through the dark glass window, like a shadow.

"Oh aye!"

"Strong as an ox, that one. She'll be out in no time." The man smiled at her as he followed his mate into the cab.

The ambulance was driven off down the towpath, slowly splashing through puddles, then it turned onto the road and was gone. Helen gazed after it, holding the key in her hand. Even if Miss Brady doesn't like me much, she thought, she must trust me.

"Hello, Cobbler," she called, going to the edge of the canal. "Come on."

But the swan stayed on the far bank and would not come to her. Only the empty barge was left, with paint peeling from the bright roses on the cabin door.

"You're very quiet, our Helen," said Mum.

"They've taken Miss Brady to hospital."

"She'll be alright."

Helen looked at the place on the piano where Peter's photographs had been. "I think she was scared."

"Scared? That one? Never!" said Dad, pulling on his wellingtons.

"I think she was," Helen said again, quietly. "When she gave me the key, her hands were shaking."

"You can go and visit her, love." Mum smiled at Helen. "Anyway, old people's hands do shake. It's just something that happens."

"Come on," said Dad. "Let's go and dig up some worms."

21

"There's no point. There isn't a badger on the barge any-more. There isn't anyone," and although she had not meant to, Helen began to cry. Hot tears prickled between her fingers and stung her chin, and the sobs were like someone stamping the breath from her chest.

"Oh, Helen . . ." Dad stared at her.

"Go away!" Helen cried. "Go away! Go away!"

She lay awake in the dark, watching the moon through the window. Mum and Dad were asleep. The house was still. She could feel the emptiness of the barge beyond the deserted streets. Empty, with only the moon to keep it company on the silver water.

It was as if she was the only person awake in the whole of the sleeping town.

At last she crept out of bed and went to Peter's room. She did not switch on the light, just stood in the doorway, looking. The same moon was in the window – but the bed was stripped to the mattress. The walls were bare. The wardrobe stood open and the moonlight glinted on the empty coat-hangers. There was nothing left at all. Dad had burnt everything.

She had to be sure. She went to the chest of drawers and pulled open the top drawer. There was nothing in it. No-thing but the pattern on the lining paper.

Quietly, she slid open all the drawers, and, finally, at the back of the bottom one, she found the photographs, face down in their frames. She knelt and stared at their backs, knowing what they were. Then, one by one, she picked them up. She could hardly remember what Peter looked like, until she took the photographs to the window.

The moon sailed among clouds, like the swan among the leaves which floated on the canal. By its light she looked at Peter's face. Three different faces, but all Peter, all the same, growing older.

The silence was worse than Peter not being there anymore. It was like a monster of silence that had nothing to do with her brother at all. She and Mam couldn't go on not mentioning him. Sometimes there was nothing else to speak about. It was like anything else, she thought. The more you aren't supposed to do something, the more you want to.

Her fingers made steamy prints on the cold glass. Muddled up in her thoughts was the face of Miss Brady as the ambulance door closed, and the different silence in which they had all knelt last night, watching the badger play.

You can't pretend to forget, she thought. You just blooming can't! Silent as a shadow in the sleeping house, Helen crept downstairs. She went to the piano and, very carefully, put the framed photographs back where they had always been. Then she stepped back and looked at the pictures, both Peter's and hers. Both of them, grinning for the school photographer.

And now the sitting-room looked once more as it had always looked, just because those three photographs were back, leaving no room for gaps or for the empty spaces where Peter had been.

A creak upstairs made her jump. She hid behind the door. But no one came. After one last look, she hurried quietly back to bed and, as she pulled the cold sheets over her shoulders, the moon slid from her window and left her in the quiet, silver dark.

She could not eat her breakfast. She was waiting for Dad to notice. And so was Mum. Mum's face was grey as old newspaper, but she said nothing. When Mum had come in from the kitchen she had almost dropped the teapot, then she had gone to the piano and picked up every photograph and put it down in the exact place where it had been before the policeman had come to the door to tell them about Peter. She had not said a word. She had hardly looked at Helen, and, with a cold shock, Helen suddenly realised that her mam hoped that Dad had put the pictures back.

But the funny thing was, Dad did not notice at all. He ate his toast, drank his tea, kissed Mum and hurried off to work.

When the front door closed, Helen said, "Mam, I put the pictures back." She thought her Mam would be angry.

"You?"

"Yes."

They were silent for a bit, looking at each other.

"Thank you, love." And that was all Mum said on the subject. "Now, hurry up, Helen. You'll be late for school."

Even at tea-time, Dad did not notice. Neither she nor Mum mentioned it.

"I've bought some grapes for you to take to Miss Brady," said Mum.

"Ta, Mum." But Helen wasn't sure she wanted to go to the hospital anymore.

"You'll have to get a move on. Visiting's from seven to eight strict. And mind you come straight home."

She didn't have much choice about going after that. The hospital was not far from Alfred Street, just up the hill, past the canal.

From the outside, the hospital looked like a cross between a prison and a church, with bars on the windows and a clock on the tower. Inside, there were green floor tiles, a smell of chemicals, and a man who told her to go to 'Female Geriatrics'.

"What does that mean?" asked Helen.

"Batty old bags!" said the man and winked at her.

Helen looked at him. She decided she did not like him at all. It must have shown in her face because the man suddenly stopped grinning like an ape and pretended to be looking for something on his desk.

She followed the signs to 'Female Geriatrics' until she came to a ward full of beds. Other visitors were already inside, sitting on chairs. They were mostly Mum and Dad's age, talking very quietly and holding the frail hand of an old woman.

At first she could not see Miss Brady. Nervously, she made her way down the aisle between the rows of beds, then she caught sight of the black and grey hair, streaked like the badger, resting on the white pillow.

"Hello!" she said.

24

Miss Brady's eyes were shut. Her skin looked as if it might tear on the sharp cheekbones. For a horrible moment Helen thought Miss Brady was dead.

"Good Lord!" whispered Miss Brady, opening her eyes. "You came after all!"

"Yes. Mam said to bring you these."

"Grapes?" Miss Brady struggled to sit up, but sank down again. "Can't bear them. Nasty pippy things. You eat them, girl. But say thank you to your mother, all the same."

"Alright." Helen sat on the edge of the hard chair, holding the bag of grapes so tightly that juice began to ooze through the paper. She did not know what to say. And she was pretty certain that Miss Brady wouldn't want her to hold her hand, like the other visitors were doing.

"It's horrible in here . . ." she said quietly, after a moment, looking round.

Miss Brady laughed in a croaky whisper. "Damn right it is! Just what I told that Sister. Devil of a place, I told her. It's like being put to bed in a public lavatory! All white tiles, disinfectant and bad smells."

Helen was startled. She grinned. "Bet that made her mad!"

"It certainly did." Miss Brady laughed louder. "Here, Helen. Give me a hand to sit up. They've pumped me so full of anaesthetic I'm as weak as a kitten."

Helen put the grapes on the locker and helped to haul Miss Brady up onto the pillows. She was heavier than she looked. Helen caught sight of Sister glaring at them from the far end of the ward. "Look out! She's watching!" she hissed in Miss Brady's ear.

"Hmmph! Let her watch. I've met her type before, but mostly they carry little sticks under their arms and shout at soldiers who've forgotten to polish their buttons. It'll take more than her to put the wind up Constance Brady, I can tell you!"

Helen and Miss Brady were sneaking looks at the nurse, like a couple of conspirators. Then Helen remembered what Miss Brady had said about not liking people, and she stopped smiling. "I wish you did like me a bit."

The old woman stopped smiling as well. "You'll do, Helen Fisher. You'll do."

"I didn't want to come tonight. But I'm glad I did now. Me dad thought you were great as well. It was the first time I seen 'im laugh since Peter got killed."

Miss Brady frowned. "Peter?"

"Oh," said Helen. She had not meant to say anything about Peter. "Me brother. He got knocked off his motorbike in April . . ."

They were quiet for a moment. Helen was glad. She did not want Miss Brady to say, 'Oh, I'm so sorry,' in her posh voice, like some of the teachers at school had said.

"So now there's just you."

Helen nodded. She had not talked to anyone about Peter. It was too hard. She felt she was only supposed to say nice things, but sometimes the things she felt weren't nice at all. "Sometimes I could blooming kill him for dying!" It just slipped out. It sounded so daft that both of them burst out laughing. Some of the other visitors turned and stared at them.

"I expect you could," said Miss Brady. "Silly thing to do at his age. Should have known better."

"Yes. Only . . . Well, sometimes I think me dad wishes it was me who had got killed and not him . . ."

"Why?"

"Oh, I dunno." Helen shrugged. "He thought Peter was so good. Going to Grammar School and that."

Miss Brady frowned until the lines on her face were almost black. "But he's still got you."

"Oh, I'm just a girl."

The old woman's hand shot out and caught Helen by the wrist. It was like being bitten. Helen jumped, alarmed. Miss Brady's eyes were like two bits of blue glass. "Just a what? Oh, Helen Fisher, you'll not do at all! The devil you won't, if I hear you say that!"

"But . . ." Helen tried to tug her hand free. "But . . ."

"But nonsense! You listen to me, just-a-girl, you'll have to sort your poor old dad out good and proper, d'you hear? Moping about. Crying over spilt milk."

26

Now Helen was angry. More of the visitors were looking at them. "Peter isn't spilt milk!"

Miss Brady let her go. "Isn't he? Well, perhaps you're right."

A bell rang at the end of the ward. Visiting time was over.

"Have I upset you, girl?"

Helen shook her head. "I'll come tomorrow."

"I'd like that, Helen."

They looked at each other, smiling again.

"Before you go, will you do somethin' for me?"

"Yes."

"Just feel the bottom of the bed – make sure I've still got two feet, will you?"

Helen thought Miss Brady was joking. She poked the bedclothes with her hand. "Yep! I think you have."

"Thank Heaven for that," murmured Miss Brady as if she meant it.

"You have. I can feel them."

"Good. Until tomorrow then."

"Tarra."

"And how's your Miss Brady then?" asked Dad when she went in. Mum was out. On Monday nights she taught adults to read – people who had not learnt while they were at school. That was something else she had started doing since Peter died.

"She hates it in there."

"I bet she does." Dad laughed quietly.

"She told the Sister it was like going to bed in a public lavatory!"

"Did she now? She's a rum old stick, and that's a fact."

Helen was standing by the piano, taking off her coat. "Don't tell me mam, but she said she hated grapes an' all."

Dad started to laugh out loud – then, suddenly, he stopped. He was staring over Helen's shoulder. At the photographs. It was as if he had been punched in the throat. His mouth was still open, but he made no sound at all.

Spilt milk, thought Helen. She was frozen to the spot. Spilt milk! Spilt milk! She wanted to shout it.

She could see Peter's face in the pupils of Dad's eyes. It was just a reflection, a trick of light. It was terrible. Like a ghost.

Any moment now, Peter would come banging through the front door with his helmet swinging from one hand by the strap, and fish and chips in newspaper in the other, yelling, *"Mam! Is it alright if I stay at Gary's? He's having a party. Hoy, Helen Fisher, ger off me chips!"*

It was worse than a ghost.

"Where's the tomato sauce?"

"Why don't you shut your mouth and open your eyes? Then you might see it's on the table."

"How's the bike?"

"Great, Dad! It's really great. Me and Gary had a race down Broadway. Couldn't see him for dust! Do you want a chip?"

"Well, you be careful, our Peter."

"Yes, Dad."

"Dad?" said Helen. "Dad?"

He shut his mouth. He closed his eyes. He opened them and looked at her.

"I put the pictures back."

"You?"

"Yes," said Helen. "Me."

"But why?" whispered Dad.

"Because," said Helen. "I could hardly remember what Peter looked like."

Dad stared at her as if she was hurting him. Then, very slowly, he nodded. "When I made the bonfire . . ." he began. His voice sounded like someone else. "When I burnt all his things . . . Do you know, that's what I kept trying to remember. Our Peter. I thought I was going daft, Helen . . . Our Peter. He looked like that . . . Aye. Well, well . . ."

"Goodnight, Dad." Just before he started crying she crept away. And this time they were real tears, not the silent deadly ones of the last six months. Helen sat on the stairs, with her face in her hands, listening, until Mum came in through the front door. Then she ran to her.

"Dad's crying."

"Oh," gasped Mum. She put her arms round Helen and hugged her close. "Thank God for that!"

4

THEY WERE let out of school at lunch time the next day, because the teachers were on strike. Instead of going straight home, Helen went to the barge. It was a chilly afternoon. Behind the trees the sky was grey and flat as concrete.

At breakfast Mum said Dad had cried all night. He had still been asleep when Helen left the house.

"Don't fret, love," Mum had said. "That's what your dad needed, a good cry."

A good cry, Helen thought as she unlocked the cabin door. A good cry. How odd it sounded, when you thought about it.

It was as if Dad had been away for a very long time, and only a good cry would bring him back.

The swan came gliding to the barge, looking for bread.

"Hello, Cobbler," said Helen. She could see his big webbed feet moving slowly beneath the oily surface of the canal. She ducked down into the cabin and went to the cupboard by the sink. There was half a loaf of stale bread.

"Here, Cobbler, come on . . ." she called going back up on deck. Three gulls flew down and bobbed on the water beside him, lunging for the bread she threw. Watching them, Helen had a strange feeling of calm, of waiting. Although the day was as dull as the bottom of a pan, somehow everything seemed to stand out very clearly. The swan, and the gulls. The trees and the bridge. And the Town Hall clock above the roofs of the town.

For a long while she watched them. Then she went back inside. In the same cupboard, at the bottom, she found two plastic bin-liners. Bad Bill would not come home. He no longer needed his nest of straw. First she took off her coat, then she found everything she needed.

She worked until it was almost dark. Although the calor gas had been switched off, she found the gas bottle and turned it on again, so she could boil the kettle. Having swept up all the straw and the foam from the ripped cushions, she found a bucket, poured in hot soapy water, and washed everything. She even picked up a few dead worms, like hard brown shoe-laces, and dropped them in the canal.

Although the barge was full of shelves and lockers, cupboards and drawers, Miss Brady did not seem to own very much. Just some clothes and books, tools and tins, a few bottles and photographs. Two of the photographs were of the badger, and one was very old, of a girl with a pointed nose and ringlets, holding a cat. You could tell by the nose it was Miss Brady. Helen put it in her coat pocket to take to the hospital. At last, when the barge was clean, she turned off the gas, locked the door, and went home.

"Where's Dad?"
"Still in bed, fast asleep."
"Is he alright?"
Mum smiled. "Yes, love. I think he is."

"Helen," said Miss Brady, when she got to the hospital. "It's war!"
"War?"
"War!" said Miss Brady, glaring down the ward to where the Sister stood. "She's confiscated my jacket. Won't let me get up. Says I'm to lie still till I'm better. Better behaved, she means. Likes her geriatrics to leave feet first, saluting, very stiffly!"
"What a mean old blighter!" said Helen.
"Exactly. Now listen, Helen Fisher. If you do this one thing for me, I might just alter my entire view of humanity."
"What?" said Helen, blinking.
Miss Brady laughed like a crow. She looked better. She looked as sly as a pirate. "I want you . . ."
"Yes?"
"To kidnap me," Miss Brady hissed.

"Kidnap you!"

"Shhh! Yes."

Helen leaned closer. The visitors were looking at them again.

"You'll have to come at lunch time. About one, if you can. They let me sit in a wheelchair and watch TV then. Some visitors come and take folks for a push round the car park. Well, you come and take me for a push down the towpath!"

"You really mean it?"

"Course I do. What do you say?"

Helen glanced at the Sister.

"Well? Will you?"

"Alright," whispered Helen. "Alright, I will. Anyhow, I've cleaned up the boat today for you."

"Well done. Tomorrow, then, if it's fine."

Helen nodded.

"Oops! Hush, here she comes."

"Comfortable?" said the Sister, stopping at the foot of the bed.

"Quite," said Miss Brady, and smiled like a gargoyle.

"Good. Good." And the Sister smiled back at her as if she had a mouthful of sour apples. Then she walked back to the cubicle and rang the bell.

"Oh!" Helen suddenly remembered. "I found this picture of you." She got it out of her pocket.

"Keep it. Ugly sort of brat, wasn't I? Still, it might bring you luck."

"See you tomorrow then."

"About one o'clock, remember."

When she got to the door, Helen glanced back. Miss Brady waved to her, as if it were a secret sign – which it was.

It wasn't until she was on her way home, that she remembered school.

"We don't have to go to school tomorrow, Mam." Helen lied.

"Why not?"

"Because the teachers are on strike again."

31

Frowning, Mum went over to the mantelpiece to look for the note Helen had brought home the week before. Helen had forgotten about the note. Her hands went hot.

"Are you sure, love? It says here that they're only on strike for half a day."

"Oh yes," Helen said quickly. She wished she had said nothing now – just crept out of school at lunch time. She'd never played truant before. "They said to tell you but I forgot."

"Well, I don't know. I wish they'd let folks know about these things in good time. What will you do all day?"

Helen could hardly look up at Mum. She hated lying to her, particularly now. "Oh, I'll be alright. I'll go and see Miss Brady at lunch time, they've got special visiting in the afternoons."

"Well, I suppose you'll be alright. But I'll have something to say to your Mrs Phillips next time I see her. Really, she could have tried to let people know."

That was the trouble with lying. Once you started you just had to keep going until you were tied in a knot. Helen crossed her fingers under the table, and showed Mum the picture of Miss Brady as a girl to change the subject.

"Hello." Dad poked his head round the door. He was still in his pyjamas, and his hair was standing on end from being asleep. "Any chance of a cup of tea? I'm parched."

"You look like a hedgehog," said Helen.

"That's because I'm going into hibernation, love. Wake me up come spring. Night-night."

"Come,ye thankful people, come,
    Raise the song of harvest-home," sang Helen as she ran along the towpath next morning. The first frost of autumn was melting on the fallen leaves, and curls of vapour licked over the canal.

"Me aunty Mary
    Had a canary
    Up the leg of her drawers!" she sang, changing tune as she jumped over a puddle. The sun looked like a red ball

thrown high above the trees. It did not matter what she sang
aloud, because inside she was singing, "Me dad's gone to
work today! Me dad's had a shave and gone to work! Me
dad's come out of hibernation – I can tell by his eyes!"

"When she farted
Down it darted
Looking for quieter shores!"

Her pockets crackled with the packet of biscuits and bag of
mints she had bought from the Co-Op, ready for when Miss
Brady and she escaped.

"Cobbler, you daft duck!" she cried when she was aboard
the barge. "Come here."

She threw him an orange cream from the packet. But it
sank without a ripple. She broke another one into small
pieces and tossed that for him, instead.

Inside the barge, it was cold. Very faintly, like a memory,
she could just smell Bill Badger. She tried to imagine where
he would be now, curled up amongst autumn leaves with his
striped head tucked against his grey stomach, snoring softly.
The thought made her quiet. She wished he was still here.
She guessed that Miss Brady would miss him, even if it was
for the best.

It was too chilly even to take off her coat. Shivering, she
went to the stove and opened the lid. Inside, there were
newspaper rolls and kindling, neatly set, and by the stove
was a green coal scuttle with roses painted on it. It did not
take long to light the fire, and she crouched by the open
mouth of the stove, putting in pieces of coal until the red
glow began to scorch her face. Soon the long cabin was
warmer.

It was the last time she would have the boat to herself. She
sat watching Cobbler through the window, pretending that
she lived on the barge, alone. It was a quiet place, and
everything in it was smaller and brighter than in their house.
There were even roses painted on the dustpan and on the
handle of the brush.

It was like a different world from Alfred Street, she
thought. You could catch fish from the canal. Perhaps you

could even find duck eggs in spring. And all winter you could sit by the stove, listening to the rain pattering on the cabin roof and hiss on the water. And when the summer came you could chug slowly away up the canal, over the aqueduct, to green fields full of cows and rabbits, and woods where badgers lived.

She remembered Dad saying to Peter, "You get your exams, lad. You don't want to spend the rest of your life in Alfred Street."

"Why not? You have."

Flames flickered like shadows, like memories, round the lid of the stove.

"Aye. Too blooming right I have. And I'm sick to the teeth of being the oily rag, son. You could be the engineer."

That was all over now. Dad had never known that Peter liked Alfred Street, that all his mates lived there, that he hated being the Grammar School boy. If he hadn't got killed, Helen thought, watching the flame-shadows, he'd have stayed. It's me that'll leave Alfred Street – and I think Dad's known it all the time.

It was like a shining silence inside her. The truth.

The Town Hall clock struck and began to play its hour tune. Quickly, she tipped some more coal into the stove, put on the lid, and glanced round, making sure everything was ready for when they got back.

When she got to the hospital the other visitors were waiting in the corridor, carrying bunches of flowers. They did not talk, but stood patiently, staring at the green tiles of the floor. Their silence made Helen nervous, although she knew they were only waiting for the bell.

Then it rang and everyone surged through the open doors, smiling now, and waving to the old people who lay in the beds.

But Miss Brady's bed was empty, neatly made, as if no one had slept in it. She stared. Her stomach went cold, as if she had swallowed a lump of ice. Then, suddenly, she remembered what Miss Brady had told her. She'd be in a wheelchair, of course! She ran down the ward to where she could see an open door leading to a small lounge.

The Sister caught her by the shoulder, "Walk, if you please. Don't want any accidents, do we?"

Right place to have them, thought Helen. "Sorry," she said. "I'm looking for Miss Brady."

"Ah, yes," said the Sister. She smiled like a needle. "You'll find her in the day room." She walked away, her heels tap-tapping on the tiles.

Helen only just managed not to stick out her tongue after the retreating blue back. She dashed into the lounge.

Miss Brady was sitting by the window, in a wheelchair, with a rug over her knees, and another over her shoulders. She was wearing her old tweed jacket over a nightie and one pink slipper on her unbandaged foot. "Helen!"

"Hello!"

"Ready?"

"Yes. And I've lit the stove."

"Good show! I've asked the sergeant-major if I could get a breath of fresh air. Had a devil of a job to persuade her."

"Do you think she suspects?"

Miss Brady shook her head. Her eyes were bright and the corner of her mouth twitched in a sly grin.

But Helen crouched down by the wheel-chair, frowning. "Are you sure you're alright? What if she's right? What if you should stay in hospital?"

"Oh poppycock!" said Miss Brady crossly.

Helen laughed. "It isn't illegal, is it? I mean, I'm up to me neck in trouble as it is. I told me mam we didn't have to go to school today because the teachers were on strike! She'll murder me when she finds out."

"Oh. I didn't mean you to lie to your parents, Helen." Miss Brady looked troubled. She obviously had not thought about school either.

"Never mind. It's too late now. Come on."

"Tally-ho!" cried Miss Brady, and every visitor in the ward turned to look as Helen pushed the chair past Sister's cubicle. But the Sister pretended not to notice.

Helen put all her weight behind the chair, and they sped towards the main doors, with Miss Brady's bandaged leg stuck out in front like a battering-ram.

"Found your granny, did you then?" The man at the desk grinned and winked at Helen.

Miss Brady and Helen both turned and looked at him, with eyes as sharp as pins.

The man's grin staggered off his face. He coughed into his hand and came and opened the door for them.

Then they were out into the cold car park. "We've done it!" cried Helen, and charged Miss Brady and the wheelchair past Casualty and Out-Patients, towards the main gate. An ambulance driver frowned at them, pushed back his cap and scratched his head.

Miss Brady was hunched like a rally driver as they trundled down King Street, the wheels clicking on the cracks in the paving-stones. Over the bridge they went, across the road, and onto the towpath by the side of the inky canal.

"Slow down, Helen!" called Miss Brady. "You'll tip me in."

"No, I won't," said Helen, just as the wheel hit a stone, and she almost did. "Ooops! Sorry!"

"There," said Miss Brady softly. They could see the barge framed by the arch of the bridge. "Now that's a sight for sore eyes . . ."

Helen stopped pushing. They were silent for a long moment, watching the white swan breasting the inky water above his own reflection. The conker trees burned in the autumn sunlight, and the painted barge rested peacefully by the bank.

"What if they come after you?"

"Oh, they probably will, Helen. But it won't do them any good."

"Will you sail away now?"

"No. No. Not until spring. Perhaps not even then. I rather like it here."

"Good," said Helen.

"Do you know? I might just nominate you for Kidnapper of the Year!"

Helen pushed the wheelchair through the puddles to the gang plank, then helped Miss Brady aboard. They left the wheelchair and the hospital rugs stranded on the bank.

"Heavenly . . ." sighed the old woman, sinking down onto the bunk. "It's warm as toast in here." She kept hold of Helen's hand. "Thank you, Helen."

"It's alright."

Miss Brady squeezed her fingers gently, then let her go. "How about a pot of tea to celebrate?"

"And I've brought you some biscuits as well." Helen brewed up. They sat by the stove drinking mugs of tea with a dash of brandy. Helen told her about the ambulance man staring at them, and they both started laughing.

They were still laughing, and Miss Brady was doing imitations of the Sister ordering the Female Geriatrics to hand over their bedpans, when they heard the heavy footsteps on the gang plank, and a knock on the cabin door.

Helen jumped. She knelt on the bunk and looked out of the window. "Oh no! There's a policeman!"

"Well, put the kettle on again," said Miss Brady. "He'll probably want a cup of tea."

Helen stared at her.

But Miss Brady called, "Come in. It isn't locked."

The ambulance driver came down the companion-way, shaking his head and trying not to smile.

"Well, close the door, young man. You're letting the cold in. Unless you're going to invite the constable aboard for a cup of tea."

"Blooming heck! You're a rum 'un," said the driver, with a sigh. "She's here, Dave!" he called. "Snug as a bug in a rug. I told them she would be."

"Absent without leave," said Miss Brady, folding her arms, and smiling like the Cheshire Cat.

Mum said nothing until Dad came in and they were all sitting down to tea. Helen kept grinning to herself, remembering the look on the ambulance man's face when Miss Brady had poured a drop of brandy into the policeman's tea.

37

"Now, our Helen," said Mum. "You've got some explaining to do."

"Pardon?"

"I met Mrs Phillips on the bus," said Mum. "On strike, my foot!"

"Helen?" Frowning, Dad looked at her.

"Oh Lord!" said Helen, and nearly burst out laughing, because that was exactly what Miss Brady would have said. But Mum and Dad were not smiling.

"Well," said Dad. "I won't have my children lying to me."

"I'm sorry," muttered Helen.

"But what did you lie for? Are you in trouble at school?"

"No, Mam."

"But you didn't go to school today, did you?"

Helen shook her head.

Mum looked exasperated. "Well, what did you do?"

"I went to the hospital."

"But you could have done that this evening," said Dad.

"No, I couldn't." Helen sighed. That was the trouble with lies – they always got you in the end. She sighed. She sucked in a deep breath and began to explain. "I had to go at lunch time – it's the only time I could kidnap her."

"Kidnap who?" Dad put his slice of cake back on the plate.

"Miss Brady, of course!" Helen told them all about it. She told them about the starchy Sister and the white tiles, and the visitors who looked paler than the patients. She did her best to explain. "So I had to go at lunch time – but it wasn't Miss Brady's fault."

When she had finished there was silence for a moment. She hung her head, staring at the table, waiting for her mam to start shouting.

But suddenly Dad began to laugh. He laughed so hard the teapot lid rattled.

"John! It's not funny!" cried Mum sharply. "John! Our Helen has been playing truant. John! It isn't funny at all!"

"Oh yes it is," wheezed Dad. "It's the funniest thing since sliced bread! Kidnapping! That old trooper! The cunning old rascal! Oh, our Helen, what will we do with you? Kidnapping." He wiped his eyes with the back of his hand. "Kidnapping's a very serious crime." He tried to make his voice serious, but caught sight of Mum and Helen staring at him and burst out laughing again.

"And then," said Helen, "she gave the policeman and the ambulance man a pound each for their trouble."

"Did they take it?" gasped Dad. He'd gone red in the face. He kept snorting like Bad Bill.

"They had to!"

"I bet they did!" croaked Dad.

"Bribery and corruption, Miss Brady said."

"Oh," sighed Dad at last, gasping for breath. "I wish our Peter had been here to hear that! He'd have split his sides. Kidnapping!" he snorted, and the teacups nearly rattled off the table.

"Oh, John!" Mum shook her head at them both, but she was smiling. There were tears in her eyes. But she was smiling.

"Come on, you two!" said Dad, grabbing his jacket from the back of the chair. "Let's take that old Badger a bottle of stout!"

As they stepped out onto the pavement, Dad was still laughing, and the October sun and the rising moon were perched like starlings on the chimneys of Alfred Street.

Reicker

For Katy

"SIEG HEIL! Sieg Heil!"

Arms outstretched in a black-line salute across the sun, mouths wide open, laughing, the two of them stood on the parapet of the bridge as the old man trudged by.

"Heil Hitler!" Sean yelled, and snapped his elbow stiff again.

"Here! I thought a German Shepherd was a kind of dog!" Martin shouted.

"Nazi! Nazi! Nazi!" They stamped the chant until they tumbled off the parapet, grinning like apes, and goose-marched up the hill behind old Reicker.

He turned on them, shaking his stick. "Go!" he barked. "Go away!"

"Woof-woof!" Martin barked back.

"Nazi! Nazi! Nazi!" Legs stiff, kicked up, the black line of their mocking salute, then a smart turn and they scattered back to the bridge, whooping. The old man stood skylined on the crest of the moor road, a stick-figure, solitary. Then he hurried out of view.

Martin wiped the sweat off his face with his arm and slouched against the warm stones of the bridge. Sean perched next to him, legs dangling over the trickle of the parched stream. Boredom came back like a headache. It was too hot. Sweat tickled Sean's ribs. And it was too still. The pressure of stillness was building up in the air, in their heads, waiting for thunder, for something to break.

"Do you reckon old Reicker really was a Nazi?"

43

Martin looked up from the water. "My dad says he was in the Luftwaffe. Got shot down or something – anyhow, he was a prisoner-of-war over at Calder Beck."

Sean frowned. He flicked a fly away from his hot face. "Why didn't he go back to Germany then, after the war?"

"Dunno. I expect they shot all the Nazis in Germany. So he stayed here." He paused, considering. "They'd be too soft to shoot him here. But I reckon they should have done."

"Bet you couldn't! Not after he'd been working up at Clegg's farm for years. You couldn't have just ordered him out of the kitchen and stood him against the shippen wall." Sean aimed an invisible rifle and spat the crack, whine, and ricochet of a bullet.

Martin pretended to duck, then he grinned. "No, I couldn't have shot him in the farmyard."

"You see," said Sean.

"I wouldn't want to scare all them innocent sheep!" He gave Sean a shove which nearly pushed him over the bridge, but yanked him safe in the nick of time. "Tell your mother I saved you!"

But Sean did not laugh. "Give over, Martin. It's too hot for mucking about."

They slumped, elbow to elbow, staring at the thin shallow stream. It looked less like real water than the mirages shimmering on the hot tarmac.

"Seriously, though," Sean said. "Do you reckon you could have shot him? Old Nazi Reicker, I mean."

"Well, he wouldn't have been old then, would he?" Martin pulled a face, thoughtful. "I'd have given him a chance – a head start. Like, a day to escape, and then I'd have gone after him. Given him a chance."

"No," said Sean. "That's worse!"

"Well," Martin protested. "At least he'd have had a sporting chance – it's more than they gave the Jews."

"A sporting chance!" Sean mimicked.

"Eh up!" Martin nudged him. "Grockles!"

A car was crawling slowly nearer, all the windows wound down, squabbling children yelling in the back seat, the radio blaring. It slowed up by them. The man leaned over his wife to the window. "Are we on the right road to Bleathwaite, lads?"

Sean put on his country-yokel face. "Ooh-ar, na' then," he drawled and looked vaguely at Martin.

Martin tried not to laugh. "Well 'ee be right in a manner o' speakin'," he drawled.

"As the crow flies," Sean added sagely.

The man's face got redder.

"Follow this here lane as far as 'ee can, then turn right, then first left, then the third turning right on your right, then second left. Can't miss it."

"Eh, wait on," Sean said, scratching his head. "Don't 'ee mean the fourth right on your left?"

The tourist glared at them. He plonked back into the driving seat and put his foot on the accelerator. The car jerked away. Three small kids turned and stared at them out of the back windscreen. Martin and Sean pretended to throw themselves off the bridge for their benefit. They landed safely among cow-parsley and bracken.

"What shall we do now?"

"Dunno."

"I wish it would thunder. Or something." Martin lay back on the hard, parched grass, his hands under his head. He looked at the glazey glare of the sky through the black fronds of bracken. "I wish we lived in London or somewhere. Somewhere where something would happen."

"What kind of thing?"

"Anything. Something. Anything."

Sean lay on his side next to him, propped on his elbow. He plucked aimlessly at the grass.

"I'm sick of this valley," Martin muttered.

Sean looked at him. "I don't know," he said. "I reckon you'd only get into trouble if you lived in London, or Leeds."

"What do you mean?" Martin lifted his head and looked at him sharply.

Sean shrugged his shoulders. "Fighting, you know. Nicking and cars and that. You know."

45

"I'm not a blooming skinhead!" Martin said.

"No. I know. I just meant you might be if you didn't live here."

Martin closed his eyes. "Don't talk daft, Sean. You know your trouble – you watch too much telly."

They were quiet in the thick heat. Flies buzzed and settled and were flicked away.

"Look," Sean pointed. "A buzzard up over the Clough."

Without opening his eyes Martin pretended to chuck a stone at it. "So what's new?"

"We could go up to the tarn for a swim," Sean suggested, sitting up. It would mean a four mile trek on the ridge of the hot moorland, but just the thought of the cool greenish water over the slate made his mouth water.

But Martin shook his head, his eyes closed.

Sean sat fidgeting, chucking bits of grass and bracken into the sluggish trickle of the stream. "What then?"

"Ah, shut up, Sean," Martin murmured. "You're like a little kid – 'What shall we do now?'" he whined, mimicking. "You'll be saying we should go and help my dad with the walling in a minute."

"Well, it'd be better than doing nowt!" said Sean angrily.

Martin opened his eyes and squinted at the silhouette of his restless friend. "You know why they don't let your kind of people be farmers?"

"Why?"

"Because when you'd finished shearing sheep you'd start shearing cows!"

"Ger on! Ger on, Blackie! Ger on, Joss!" Martin strode up Tupper's Field, waving his arms. Sean followed at his shoulder.

"What's to do with them?" he asked.

"It's this flaming thunder that won't break. Ger on, lad!" Martin side-stepped and the colt stopped, hooves spraddled, head down, snorting. Blackie trotted, shook her mane, snorted and stilled, ears flattened to her big bony skull. It gave the two ewes a chance to escape. They hesitated, turned together, then pattered through the gap in the wall with neat fleecy leaps. The two horses had been chasing the sheep mercilessly, round and round.

"They'll be alright now," said Martin. "Come on, Blackie, girl. Come on."

But the mare bucked and cantered away to the lower wall, and the big colt wheeled after. "That's three days they've been like this."

Sean pulled his damp T-shirt away from his sweaty chest and let it flop back. The sunset was frazzling over the Clough. The stillness was like a weight. You could not breathe it. Sean looked at Martin as he stood there, his hands shoved into the hip pockets of his jeans, his gaze fixed on the agitated mare. Somehow, since the summer holidays had begun, Martin had outgrown him. He could not keep up. He was standing in Martin's shadow, and it was the first coolness of the day.

"It's alright for you," Sean said as they climbed the gate.

"What is?"

"All this." Sean waved his hand in a wide gesture across the side of the Clough, the dry-stone walls cast like a net over the rough steep land. Everything they could see belonged to High Clough, Charlie Bradan's farm. Charlie Bradan was Martin's dad.

"What do you mean?"

"Oh, I dunno. Nothing." Sean kicked up dust on the steep track to the farm.

"Come on?" said Martin.

"Well, you've got it all settled. You've got the farm. You don't even need exams. Me, I've got to have them."

"Ah, rubbish," said Martin. "What if I don't want to be a flaming farmer!"

"Well, what do you want to be?"

"Dunno." Martin shrugged. It was obvious he had never thought about it. "Could go into the army, I suppose."

"You don't understand," Sean said, trying to explain. His mum and dad lived in the last bungalow on the edge of town. Dad was a teacher. Mum was a nurse. They had nothing to leave him. Only education.

But Martin did not look interested. He was thinking about the horses and the gap in the wall where the sheep had got in. His dad had said he was going to rebuild that section this morning.

Sean was silent, half angry with Martin, and half knowing that it would be useless to try and explain what he meant. Once he had left school he would have no claim on this land, this lane, like Martin had. He would be a tourist, a grockle. But Martin always wanted to be somewhere else. Martin's legs had grown half a stride longer since Easter. Sean had to hurry an extra step every three to keep up.

Behind the farm, the Clough was like the flank of an animal in the last light of the day. They heard the land-rover growling to ignition as they came into the yard. Martin's dad switched off the engine. "Martin!"

"Yes?"

They went over to the battered vehicle. Charlie Bradan shook his head.

"Get in, your mam's fretting for thee."

"I've done nowt!"

"I know," said Martin's dad , opening the land-rover door. "I didn't mean it that way. Hello, Sean."

"Hello, Mr. Bradan."

"Come on, you two. We've got trouble on our hands. You'd best ring your mam and dad, Sean."

"Oh, It's O.K. They know where I am."

Charlie Bradan pushed open the farmhouse door. "Aye, but that was this morning and this is tonight."

They ducked under his big arm.

"Oh, hello love," said Charlie Bradan as Kit Bradan, Martin's mum, hurried into the hallway. "They're here."

"Thank goodness for that!" she sighed. "The police have just rung to say can they use our place as an emergency base."

"Of course they can. Now you two, get your suppers – we've got work to do."

"Mum?"

"Sean! I was getting worried," he heard her say down the telephone.

"It's alright. I'm up at Martin's."

"Well, stay there, and your dad will collect you. I've got to go to work. I'm on night duty."

"What's going on, Mum?" Sean asked. He was standing in the stone hallway. Police cars were crunching up on the gravel outside the window. Blue lights flashing, then stopping, like imitations of lightning.

"Hasn't Mr. Bradan told you?" Mum's voice was gnat-sized, metallic in his ear.

"No. He's with the police."

"Sean, there's been a terrible thing. A man in Low Calder has shot his wife, and he's got his neighbour's three year old daughter for hostage."

"He's up on the Clough?" Sean pressed himself to the wall to let Charlie Bradan and four policemen get past.

"Yes. Well, they think so. So stay where you are."

"Mum, it's alright. I won't do anything daft."

"I know you won't, love."

"Why did he shoot his wife?" Sean pressed to the wall again and more police came by. Bigger, harder men. One of them had a rifle. He could hardly believe it.

"Oh Sean," said his mum's voice. "I don't know."

"I'll wait for Dad."

"Thanks, love."

"Don't worry."

"I'll try not to." The line crackled. "That poor little mite . . ."

"Don't worry, Mum."

"Alright love. You keep out of the way. Your dad will be up soon."

"Yes, Mum."

"And Sean, this isn't a game. Do you understand me? Don't get in the way."

The policeman was questioning Martin.

Martin said, "No. No one else. Only Nazi Reicker – he's the shepherd at Clegg's – and those tourists. But no one else came past, did they, Sean?"

"No."

They heard another crunch of wheels, the scraping squeal of brakes, then the barking of police alsatians. Mittsie and Tess, the sheepdogs, crawled growling across the kitchen floor.

"It's alright, Mr. Bradan," said the policeman. "They won't go after your livestock."

"Come-by," Charlie Bradan murmured, and the sheep-dogs came to his heel. "I'll keep them in."

"Aye," said the policeman. "That's best. Eh, Mr. Bradan, it's a bad do."

"You're sure he's armed?" said Mrs Bradan, bringing mugs of tea.

"Pretty sure."

"Young Mattie Fiddler, who'd have thought it," she said. "He was always such a quiet lad."

"Now then," said Charlie. The room was hot and blue and strange with the policemen in it, sipping tea. "Remember on my land you've got the old mines – shafts and tunnels. I've done my best to fence them, but we still lose the odd ewe. I'll try to make a map if it's any help. Only, on a bright night like this you can't see anything because you think you can see everything."

"No. There's no time for map-making, Mr. Bradan."

Sean went to sit by Martin. Martin's face was tense. His eyes were quick and bright, taking in the faces, uniforms, guns.

"Ready then?" said the policeman. "Sorry, Mrs. Bradan, it's going to be a long night."

Martin said suddenly, "I'll come too."

"No . . ." Mrs Bradan started, alarmed. The policeman frowned.

"He's right," said Charlie Bradan. "My lad knows the Clough like the back of his fist. He's not a kid anymore. I'm sorry, Kit, but there's a little lass up there."

"Well, we could do with all the help we can get. O.K. You two had better come."

As Martin jumped to his feet, his mum grabbed his arm. "You do exactly what the police say, Martin."

"Yes, Mam. Come on, Sean."

They followed the men out into the pale moonlit yard. Sean glanced back down the lane, thinking of his dad. The hot night buzzed and crackled with radios and the coming storm.

"It's like being in a film," Martin hissed, as the men were split into groups.

"It's weird," Sean breathed back. It was hard to believe it was happening at all.

They were put with five officers. He recognised one – Sergeant Greenhall – and a certain shock passed through Sean as he saw that even old Greeny was wearing a shoulder-holster across his chest.

"Right lads," said Greeny, in a tone that suggested he would rather not have had them with him. "Keep up, keep quiet, and keep your heads down."

"I know Mattie Fiddler," Martin said, as they went through the gate. "He plays for the darts team."

"Oh aye," said Greeny. "So I expect you knew he was going to blow his wife's head off."

Martin shut up. They followed the dog-handler in the lee of the stone wall, as the alsatian sniffed its way across the cropped turf.

"German Shepherd," Martin whispered, nodding at the dog. Moonlight glinted in the corner of his eye.

Sean thought of the things they had shouted after old Reicker, and although he huffed a quiet laugh in reply, somehow it did not seem funny any more.

2

THE CLOUGH loomed over them, the stars of the Plough rose in the black sky beyond. It was darker now and cooler, and the sweat prickled cold on their faces as they followed the sheep track up the steep slope. The bracken fetched up almost to their shoulders in places, and the bitter brown scent of it thickened the air.

"Hey," Martin whispered to Greeny. "There's an old shepherd's hut a bit on. It's still got half a roof."

A rapid exchange passed between the officers. The dog-handler nodded. Greeny passed on the information over his radio. The radio voice crackled back. The sound seemed very loud in the still night air.

"Thanks, lad. How much further?"

Martin reckoned it. "About quarter of a mile, then over the wall."

"Right. Keep low and quiet. When we get there you stay back, stay down by the wall, and don't shift till I say. Right?"

"Right!" said Martin. He glanced at Sean. Sean was quiet. His legs ached with the steep climb. All of them were panting softly.

Sean whispered, "Do you think they'll shoot him?"

"Dunno. They might have to."

Sean also knew who Mattie Fiddler was. He had seen him in the Hare and Hounds Hotel when he had been for supper there with his mum and dad. A young man, one eye closed, the tip of his tongue touching his top lip as he aimed for a double on the darts board. It didn't make sense. Soldiers and criminals were one thing, but not somebody you'd actually *seen*, whose name was familiar, who only lived a few miles down the road . . .

"Do you think it'll be on the news?" whispered Sean, frowning in the dark.

"Yes. Fame at last!" Martin hissed back, grinning.

But that was not what Sean had meant. It had suddenly struck him that almost all murderers had next-door-neighbours, lived in ordinary streets, in ordinary places like Low Calder, Macclesfield, Leeds.

"I hope we're the ones that find him," Martin whispered a moment later. And, although Sean nodded, somewhere he began to hope they were not.

"What's the matter?" Martin murmured. They were crouched behind the wall. It seemed an age since the police had left them, though they knew one of the officers was just the other side of the wall. The waiting was worse than the silence.

"Nothing."

"I wish I could see what's going on." Martin began to rise, but Sean grabbed his arm and pulled him down.

"Don't be bloody daft!" he hissed sharply. His whisper seemed loud. They froze, listening. Clouds of invisible midges filled the bracken. A mosquito whined close to their faces and Martin brushed at his cheek with his hand.

"What if they've just left us here? I wouldn't put it past Greeny."

Sean shook his head. Their eyes had grown so accustomed to the darkness that they could see each other almost clearly.

Then they heard the clatter of stones as one of the men clambered back to them. Instinctively, they flung themselves against the wall.

"Come on," the man said. "There's nothing here."

Sean's shoulders ached with crouching and tension. They scrambled over the wall and hurried up the slope to the dark shape of the ruined bothy.

They could hear the faint trickle of the stream in a gully on their left, where mountain ash lurched at cliff hanging angles and a fallen holly combed the water. There was a vague sickening stench of a dead sheep somewhere close by in the bracken.

Sean had never climbed the Clough in the dark. The night was edged with the unbroken storm. He imagined Mattie Fiddler crouched among the stream boulders, his hand across the little girl's mouth, watching them, with the moon in the whites of his eyes. The skin crawled on his arms and shoulders. He stayed close by Martin as the radio crackled and they waited to move on.

"Your dad's at the Bradan's," Greeny said to Sean. "Wanting us to take you back."

"Oh no!"

"Don't worry, lad," Greeny grinned, hard, not humorous. "We've not got time for baby-sitting – or passengers. Come on."

They began to climb again, following the wolfish muzzle of the dog.

"Charlie says there's a shaft up here."

Martin nodded. He was striding slower, heavier, tired. "It's fenced up. We did it at Easter. There's a tunnel, but the roof's caved in. It doesn't go far. It's where we found that haversack last summer, Sean."

"Oh, I remember."

"There isn't a path anymore. Least, not this time of year. You've got to go through the bracken."

"Can you find it?"

"I think so."

Suddenly they all stopped. The alsatian sniffed back and forth, back and forth across the path. It began to wag its big feathery tail. Sean's mouth went dry. Martin looked at him. The slow, happy sinister tail of the dog and its snuffling muzzle struck coldness in both of them. Unexpected. Real. And the night tightened one more turn. They were all frozen, poised, watching the lowered snout, the black wagging tail. The silence was like a shout.

Then the dog trotted on, patient on the leash, and its handler shrugged. A false alarm. They climbed on. Martin kept by Sean's side now. They went slower.

Two ewes, startled, pranced to their feet from under the wall. They stared at the strangers with their goatish eyes, then bounded away. The bracken cracked and rustled as they vanished. The dog hardly looked at them. It was trained to hunt men.

Now they were moving above the bracken, under the screes, where once a great glacier had ground out the edge. There were boulders here, all shapes and sizes. And every boulder seemed to have eyes and a gun. If you looked at a stone too long in the darkness it seemed to move, to shimmer and tremble, like a man crouching. And now there were no walls to keep to, or duck behind. It was hard to imagine the other search parties less than a mile away on Clough Top, or Widow's Jump. They seemed so alone. Even in daylight the Clough always got bigger as you climbed it.

"Where's this shaft then?" Greeny asked.

Martin stopped. "We must have passed it."

Sean could see him frowning, trying to get his bearings. "We'd have seen," said Sean thoughtfully, "if someone had gone through the bracken today. They'd have flattened a path."

"Thank you, Sherlock," said Greeny in that hard voice. "Come on. We'll have to double back. Lead on, Macduff."

Now Martin was up in front with the dog as they crab-crawled sideways and down on the flank of the Clough. Sean trailed behind, angry. It isn't 'Lead on, Macduff', he thought over and over, staring at the black broad back of the sergeant. It's 'Lay on, Macduff, and damn'd be him that first cries Hold, enough!' They were doing *Macbeth* in English. He had begun to hate Greeny, with his hard clever voice. And he hated the piggy whistle of the man's breath as he clambered along in front of him.

"Down there," Martin said, pointing. Then a great blue flicker lit the fell side, and they saw everything in strobe-light, so that the after-image stuck on their eyes like a photograph. They blinked darkness. No thunder came. Then another sheet of lightning shocked the sky, and an imprint of everything they saw stayed with them.

The mouth of the old mine, blue and grey and black, with the fence-posts and barbed wire, was twenty feet below them. The wire was twisted and down. The posts askew. They blinked in the after-blindness of the electric storm – but all of them had seen. A section of wire was twisted and crushed down – big enough to let a man through.

"Down!" Greeny grabbed Sean and almost knocked him flat. He spraddled on the mountain side. If they could see then so could a watcher. And Sean was afraid, afraid of the cracked sky where no thunder followed, and afraid of the twisted gap in the wire. And the fear was like a bucket of icy water thrown over his back in the hot stifling night. Every-thing was super-real. All his senses were peaking and charged in a way he had never known. Martin wriggled back beside him. When the next flash came they tried to shelter each other, and it seemed the Clough bucked, and they shoved into the shelter of each other's shoulders, like soldiers when a shell explodes over their heads.

Sean gasped.

"Scared?" Martin's whisper was hot on his neck.

"Aren't you?"

"A bit. I thought I'd been shot!"

"Do you think he's in there?"

"Don't get excited, you two," Greeny muttered close by. "We've as much chance of finding him as we have of finding Father Christmas. You don't really think they'd have let you kids go where they expected danger?"

So that was it, Sean thought. Old Greeny was fuming because he might miss the action.

Another great sheet of lightning spat over the Clough as the officers made their way down to the mine. Sean and Martin lay still, their heads propped on their hands, watching, as the electric storm cracked and danced, silent and sudden, illuminating the slopes. It was like watching a series of still photographs – each image of the dog and the men and the mine staying with them in the darkness until the next flash showed the police nearer to the old workings. The dog went in first, then the police marksmen, one after the other, covering each other, and, finally, Greeny. The hillside was empty in the next split-second glare. Martin rolled onto his side and sighed. "I wish it would thunder," he said. "I hope Dad's O.K."

"My dad'll be furious," Sean said, peering down at the mine. "Mum wanted me to stay at the farm until he came."

Martin yawned. His jaw made a little dry cracking sound. "It's not like this in films," he muttered. "In films we'd find Mattie Fiddler and that."

Sean laughed softly. The lightning seemed to be moving away, but the air still prickled with it. As he sat up, the sleeve of his jersey brushed against Martin's and a tiny blue spark snapped between their arms.

"What's taking them so long?"

"They've probably stopped for a fag."

"What time do you think it is?"

"Must be nearly midnight," said Martin. The tension was ebbing away, and a vague sense of disappointment was creeping over both of them.

Sean closed his eyes, yawning, and opened them. "God!" He sat bolt upright. "Look at the Clough!"

Martin jerked round. Above them, all along the ridge of the fell, ran a thick blue glitter, like an outline drawn in blue frost. It made the Clough look weird and alien, like a moonscape in a science fiction film.

"It was worth it," Martin whispered, "just for that," as the weird light began to fade. "Must be static, or something."

But Sean was staring at something else. Something small and moving and black. He touched Martin's arm, hardly sure what he was seeing, his eyes still dazzled by the charged air. "Martin . . ."

And Martin saw it too. A figure moving slowly down the boulder field towards them, humpy and awkward, carrying something in its hand.

Sean glanced round, but there was no sign of the police at the mouth of the mine. It was too dark to see properly. And they dared not move. Slowly, so slowly that it made their bodies ache to do it, they lowered themselves flat again to the stony turf. They were alone. Twenty yards separated them from the mine.

"He's still got his gun," Martin said, so quietly that the sound seemed to come from inside Sean's head. Then they heard a faint childish wail followed by the deep low murmur of a man's voice. The sound was so far away and small that it was hard to tell when it stopped and only the murmur and babble of the mountain stream was left.

"We've got to tell them," said the voice in Sean's head which was Martin's.

Sean nodded without moving a muscle. And whether it was fear or courage, a kind of hard coldness made him ready to move.

"No," Martin whispered, louder. "Stay here. Don't move." He pressed his hand on Sean's back, pushing him down, then he was sliding away on his belly, creeping on his elbows, with hardly a sound. Sean was alone. Time stopped.

The figure was coming slowly closer. He heard the skitter of dislodged stones as the man skirted the scree, and he felt the empty unprotective air between them, where all sound would travel. The rustle of Martin in the bracken seemed louder than gunshot. He winced.

Somehow, he knew without looking that a police marksman was coming up behind him, as if some other sense was at work – something more than hearing alerted him. The man was beside him, squinting down the sights of a rifle. "Slowly," he murmured, in a voice that was firm, almost hypnotic, "Very slowly, Sean. I want you to wriggle back behind that big rock. Do you understand? Very slowly. Very quietly, Sean."

"The little girl . . ." Sean whispered. His arms and body were pinned to the side of the Clough with their own weight and he could not budge.

"Now," hissed the marksman.

But not a muscle would move. And now a new sound travelled through the still midnight air. A deep soft voice lurching in song. Soft and cracked and out of key.

"He's drunk," murmured the marksman to himself. "Now, Sean. Go!"

Then, like the crack of a whip, time started again. Sean leapt to his feet. "Reicker! Reicker!" he shouted and ran towards the man.

"Liebchen mein . . ." the song broke off. And all hell was being let loose behind them. The police were running. The dog bounded past and began to bark and growl. The child shrieked.

"Reicker! It's only Reicker!" Sean cried as the marksman threw him down. He saw in a horrible blink of stopped time the dog leaping up and the old shepherd lifting the child above his head against the stars.

Then there was a sharp shout from the dog-handler, and flashlights, and old Nazi Reicker was surrounded, with the screaming child still held high over his head, blinded by the sudden beam of the powerful torches.

Sean had to stay where he was – head down, sitting in the grass, winded. He felt sick.

He heard Reicker say, "She was on the Clough. So. I find her on the Clough, crying and falling. Lost, yes? I bring her down."

Radios were crackling and buzzing and the child's howl became a sobbing whimper.

"You O.K.?" Martin bent over him.

"I thought they were going to shoot Nazi Reicker!"

"How did you know it was Reicker?" Martin crouched on his heels.

"He was singing. German. I just knew it was! I'm O.K. now." He looked up. "Did the dog get him?"

"No. I don't think so. You scared everybody!" Martin grabbed his arm and helped him to his feet. No one was interested in them now. They had found the child, Emma.

Emma's face was pressed into Reicker's donkey-jacket. "Go 'way," she wailed as Greeny tried to take her, thrusting her small hand at him. "Go 'way." Now the night was all noise and relief. The old man was standing in the centre, patting the little girl's back. His face was stern and grey as a rock.

Reicker had to carry Emma all the way back down to the farm. She screamed if anyone else tried to take her. Reicker had found her wandering on the ridge of the Clough, crying, but he had seen no one else. And she was too little to be able to tell them anything, and too scared.

Martin and Sean scrambled after the men, staggering with tiredness. Not speaking. Sometimes Martin stopped to help Sean over gates and walls, realising he had been badly shaken. Once, when they rested, Reicker looked at them in the starlight. His eyes were like two pale stones, and the scar on his left cheek was like a black gully in his hard face.

At last they tumbled into the bright kitchen of the farm-house. Emma's mother was there, her face swollen and streaked with crying. And Sean's dad was there, pale and anxious and tall. But Charlie Bradan was still up on the fell, and so, perhaps, was Mattie Fiddler, although there had been a report that he had been seen at West Cloughton, and another report of a car being stolen from Hayton's farm, which was only a mile from Clough Bottom.

Sean went to his dad. "Sorry."

"Well, you've found her, safe and sound."

A policewoman helped Emma's mum out of the farm-house. She was crying. Little Emma was clinging to her cardigan, not crying any more, her thumb in her mouth.

The grandfather clock in the hallway struck two.

"Come on, young-feller-me-lad," said Sean's dad, putting his arm round Sean's shoulders. "Bed. If that's alright with you."

The police officer nodded.

A few minutes later they were turning into the drive of the bungalow.

"Dad . . ." said Sean.

"What's the matter? You should be proud of yourself. But we'll not tell Mum about you jumping up, eh?"

"It's not that," Sean said. "It was Nazi Reicker's face – when the dog jumped at him. I can't remember if it was dark or torches then. But I saw the look on his face . . ."

"Come on, Sean," said his dad gently. "Bed. You can tell us all about it tomorrow."

3

BUT HE COULD not tell them, not even when they asked him. He could find words to describe everything apart from that moment when the alsatian leapt with bared teeth and the old man swung the child to safety against the stars. Nazi Reicker's face in that instant was etched in his mind, like a photograph taken through the sights of a gun. But he knew he could not have seen it because it was not until a split-second later that the torches were switched on. It was an expression so beyond anything he had ever experienced that he could find no words for it. No actor could have looked like that. It was the most violent, the most frightened thing Sean had ever seen.

The bright afternoon sunlight shone through the curtains. Sparrows twittered in the gutter. All the bedclothes were on the floor and he lay, still in his jeans, on the mattress, sweating.

"I've left the phone off the hook," he heard his mother say outside his bedroom door.

Dad's sandals clicked on the hallway tiles as he came in from the garden.

"It was that reporter again."

"Sean still asleep?" That was dad's voice.

The bedroom door opened a crack.

"What time is it?" Sean asked, lifting himself onto his elbows.

"Hello. Nearly four. Feeling O.K.?"

"Yes thanks, Mum."

Mum smiled and closed the door. "He's awake, Roger."

When he went into the kitchen Dad made him a mug of coffee. Mum sat at the table shelling peas, splitting the pods along their green seams, then pushing them with her thumb into a white bowl. They were waiting for him to tell them about last night. He did his best. About the police, and the electric storm, and the strange phenomenon which lit the Clough, and the figure coming out of the dark. But there were three things he did not tell them – about Nazi Reicker's face when the dog leapt, about him and Martin shouting after Reicker with Nazi salutes and their giddy goose-march, and about the look Nazi Reicker had given them as they stumbled down the Clough in the dark.

"Have they caught him yet?" he said, after a moment's silence.

Dad shook his head. "No. They think he might have stolen a car. But at least little Emma's alright. And," Dad added, with a forced bright smile, "so are you."

Sean could see that they were trying not to be angry with him for having gone with Martin and the police.

Although Mum's hands never stopped their quick splitting

of the pods which sent the peas rattling softly into the bowl, she kept looking at Sean, little sipping glances, as if she had to keep reassuring herself that he was safe, and the same.

"Mum," he said at last. "I did a daft thing last night. I might have got somebody killed..."

Her hands stopped their work.

"I thought they were going to shoot Reicker, so I jumped up and shouted. I thought they were going to shoot him... I don't know why I did it."

Sean saw Dad looking at him, and somehow he knew he had done the right thing to tell her before anyone else did.

"Well," she said quietly. "You couldn't help it." She began to sweep the empty pods off the table into the colander. "Last night I was on Casualty. Every time they pushed open the swing-doors I could hardly bear to look, in case it was little Emma they brought in... Well, she's safe now. At least I wasn't on duty when they brought Jean Fiddler..." She stopped herself, and hurried out of the back door to put the pea pods on the compost heap.

"What really happened, Dad?" Sean asked when she had gone.

"You were there, Sean. You know better than us."

"No. I didn't mean... Did Mattie Fiddler really blow his wife's head off?"

Dad stared at the table. In the silence a car roared past the bungalow.

"He certainly shot her. She was dead by the time they got her to the hospital."

"Why?"

"I don't know why he killed her. They'd not been married long."

"Is everyone alright at the Bradan's?"

"Oh yes," said Mum, coming back in. She looked better. "They don't think he's on the Clough any more."

"Can I go and see Martin?"

"No," said Mum slowly, looking at him. "Not today."

"Shock," said Dad, "is a funny thing. You might just feel it soon. It's a bit like 'flu."

"I'm O.K.," Sean protested. But the truth was that the heat and the night and Nazi Reicker's face had left him hollow as a straw.

For a while he sat in the kitchen with the radio on. Mum and Dad were never far away. Mum made a salad. Dad brought in a lettuce from the garden and tomatoes from the greenhouse. They went out onto the patio to eat. He and Mum had only finished building the patio a few weeks before. He had spread the sand for setting the paving-stones. She had pegged off, and smoothed it level. Now it was decorated with Dad's miniature roses and fuschia standards, and the white cast-iron table he and Dad had bought for Mum's birthday.

Swifts flew screaming low over the lawn. Thunder was still in the air, heavy and humid. Sean could hardly eat. Nothing seemed quite real. In his mind everything was dark, but on the patio everything was bright, decorative, peaceful, and the same.

Dad brought a bottle of home-made white wine from the fridge, and he filled Sean's glass without making his usual jokes about under-age drinkers.

When Mum went in, Sean said, "Was Reicker really a Nazi?"

Dad opened his mouth to answer, then he shut it again and thought, as if the look on Sean's face had made him think deeper. "That depends," he said, sipping his wine, "what you mean. He was a German and in the war, and I think he was in the German airforce, which was run by the Nazis. He might have shot some of our planes down. It was a long time ago, you know, Sean. I would only be about your age when the war was on, but my eldest brother, Michael was shot down. It's hard to forget, but it's hard to remember as well. When Michael died I never knew about Belsen or the Jews. I just knew about Michael, and my mother, your grandma, crying."

Dad was silent. Swifts screamed and swarmed over his head, twisting in wild acrobatic chases. "It seems funny to think that when Michael was only a couple of years older

than Martin Bradan he was flying bombers over
Germany . . ." He glanced at Sean, as if he was seeing him in
a new way, measuring him against the boys he had known in
his own youth who had been called up. "You see, the thing
is, Sean, I can't ever really get to know someone like him –
Reicker, I mean – though I know he's suffered – because of
my brother. I was very close to Michael. But what with the
war, and Churchill, and Hitler . . . In wars most men fight
for what they're told to believe in, I suppose. I don't blame
Reicker – I just can't see *him*." Dad stared into his glass.
"Even though it was so long ago, and best forgotten."

Sean sat with his chin in his hands. He could see shadows
in Dad's face like black leaves floating to the surface of a pool
someone has stirred with a stick. And he thought of the
things he and Martin had yelled after Nazi Reicker.

In the late afternoon the garden was sweet with the scent of
roses, humming with insects, and a new thought came to
Sean. Sometime, yesterday, at some precise moment when
he and Martin were larking about, Mattie Fiddler had shot
his wife – squeezed the trigger, and shot her, in that same,
exact moment of time. And perhaps further back still in time,
on an afternoon like this, a squadron of bombers had droned
over the valley, heading for the industrial cities. Perhaps, on
just such a hot, quiet, July evening, high above the shrill
acrobatics of the swifts, a black formation of German planes
had thrown their gliding shadows over the fields and fells and
dry-stone walls of the Clough, and Nazi Reicker had glanced
down from the cockpit and, without knowing it, seen the
tiny buildings of the farm where he would spend the rest of
his life.

"Penny for them?" said Dad, nudging him.

"I was just thinking," said Sean slowly, trying to put his
thoughts into words. He shook his head. "I was just thinking."

"Well," said Dad, "perhaps I should have offered tuppence
for them."

Sean got to his feet. "I'm going to have a shower."

"Right-ho!" Dad said. As Sean went into the living-room

through the patio doors he noticed his father watching him, his face still and thoughtful, and almost sad.

That evening they stayed on the patio, watching the stars appear over the pine trees at the bottom of the garden. The swifts were silent now. And the death of Jean Fiddler in the valley below had cast a quietness over the whole family. Dad sat on the edge of his canvas chair, his elbows on his knees, his chin resting on his steepled hands. Mum lay back in the deck chair, a cardigan round her shoulders, gazing up into the blue darkness of the sky. And Sean sat between them on the step.

A new closeness kept them silent, as if the unexpected violence in their small valley had subtly changed the whole world, and their places in it. Not one of them would easily have been able to say aloud what they were thinking at that moment.

They heard a car draw up in the drive. Then a knock on the front door. Mum started up.

"I'll go," said Dad.

They both turned and watched as Dad switched on the lights and disappeared out of view into the hallway.

"Oh, hello Charles," they heard Dad say. "Come in. We're out the back."

"Evening, Roger." Charlie Bradan and Dad came out through the patio doors.

"Evening, Sean. Mary." Martin's dad nodded at them. He was taller and broader than Sean's father, and still in his working clothes, with his shirt half open showing his broad sunburnt chest.

"Do you fancy a beer? There's some in the fridge."

"I'd not say no."

He sat on the step by Sean. "Budge up, lad."

"Have they found him?" Sean made room for Charlie's bulk.

"No, not yet. But don't fret – they will. They don't reckon he's up on the Clough now, though. Cheers!" He took the cold glass from Sean's dad.

"How's Kit?" asked Mum.

"Not so bright, Mary, if the truth be told. It's right upset her – what with the police all night, and the lads and me having to go out. She had to see Emma's mum – they brought her up to the farm, you know, when the lads found the little lass. Poor woman. What a state she was in. Still, at least Mattie Fiddler had the sense not to harm her. I expect she'll forget about it in time – she's only a babby yet. Anyway, I just thought I'd pop down and see how Sean was getting on."

"I'm fine thanks," Sean said. "Were you out all night on the Clough?"

"Aye, lad. We didn't get back till light. But it was a damn sight better after I knew you and Martin were safe and sound."

"Is there anything we can do?" Mum said.

Charlie Bradan shook his head. "There's nowt any of us can do. It's in the hands of the police. Let's just hope that Mattie has the sense to turn himself in before there's more tears shed. He's a bigger danger to himself now than to anyone else, I reckon . . . Poor Jean. She used to help our Kit on the milk-round, you know, before she got married . . ."

"But why did he do it, do you think, Mr Bradan?" Sean asked.

"I don't know, lad. It's past my imagining. He always had a devil of a temper, did young Mattie. Same as his father. We always used to say about Fiddlers, that where they were concerned it was a win, set, or barney every time."

"What do you mean?"

"Well, if Fiddlers were playing in a game they'd either have to win it, or set – you know, draw evens – or there'd be a barney, a fight. Bad losers the lot of them. And jealous with it.

"Any road up," Charlie Bradan added after a moment. "I just wanted you and Mary to know that Sean had no choice last night. Him and Martin aren't kids any more. The police needed all the help they could get."

"Oh," said Sean's dad. "We realised that. We don't blame Sean for joining in. Do we, Mary?"

"No, of course not," said Mum, but both their voices sounded less certain than Charlie Bradan's.

Sean fidgeted, then drank the rest of his wine.

"Our Martin reckons that Sean was the first to see old Reicker coming off the Clough. He was too busy gawping at the lightning."

Sean felt pleased that Martin had at least given him the credit for that. Martin could easily have said they had both seen the figure at the same time. "But Martin fetched the police out of the mine," he said, in return.

"Aye, well. He knows the Clough better than you, Sean. And as for being quiet when he wants – he could catch rabbits in his bare hands! Well, I'd best be off. Kit'll be fretting, and she's had enough to worry about as it is. Oh, by the road, we've had reporters buzzing round High Clough like flies on a cow. I've sent them packing. I don't want our Martin's ugly mug all over the front pages of the Gazette."

"I quite agree," said Sean's dad. "It's a sad enough business without the press making a meal of it."

As Charlie got up to go, Sean said, "What happened to Reicker?"

"Oh, they've taken his statement at the station. He'll be back at Clegg's now."

"Are the reporters pestering him?"

"Well, that I don't know, Sean. It's stories these press fellers are after – not the truth. And there's more story to be had from two young lads like you than from some old codger." He looked at Dad. "Mind you, if he's got any sense he'll keep his head down. It doesn't take much to stir the grudging memories of some folks in the valley. Well, goodnight."

When he had gone, Sean said, "What did Mr Bradan mean?"

Dad sighed. "It's not that many years back since the Cleggs were still getting their windows broken occasionally, by idiots who thought they shouldn't have let old Reicker stay on. Someone even painted swastikas on some of Clegg's sheep. You wouldn't credit it after all these years, would you?"

Nazi! Nazi! Nazi! They had chanted, grinning like apes, and goose-marched up the hill behind the old man. That was yesterday. Sean stared at the ornamental paving-stones between his feet.

4

THUNDER RUMBLED and echoed over the Clough. Lightning jagged across Stang Head on the far side of the valley. Sean counted, "One and two and three and four. . ." then the kettledrum clash shook Clough Bottom. Heavy drops of rain splattered the dusty yard, leaving dark rings. Then it pelted down, washing the old land-rover from dusty grey to green. The morning suddenly became cooler.

Martin and Sean were sitting on hay-bales in the doorway of the barn. Sean pulled his feet in from the rain. The water snickered and glugged over the sloping yard, the ground too hard for it to sink in. They watched the stony lane turn into a stream, then a frothing torrent. The rain stopped as suddenly as it had started, like a tap being switched off. Thunder rumbled far away, almost inaudible. After the thick heat of the last four days, the coolness was a luxury. They breathed it in.

"They still haven't caught him," Martin said, plucking a straw from the bale and twisting it round his fingers.

"Your dad reckoned he'd give himself up in the end," said Sean. He stretched out his hand so that the rain dripped from the barn roof onto his fingers. It was warm as blood, not cold as he had expected.

"Do you know what I reckon?" said Martin, suddenly sitting forward, frowning.

"What?"

"I reckon that Nazi Reicker knows where he is. I bet he's helping him escape."

Sean stared at him.

"Honest," said Martin. "I bet."

"Why should he?"

Martin shrugged. "He was a prisoner once, wasn't he? I bet he tried to escape. I wouldn't put it past him. He'd bring Emma down, then Fiddler could hide more easily. It makes sense."

"Does it heck! Don't talk daft!" Sean went quite cold. Martin was just trying to make something happen, something in which he could be involved, like in a film. "That's just stupid. You know what you are – blood-thirsty!"

Martin swung his head and looked him full in the face, with a sneering superior look. "Oh aye? I bet you anything you like. A tenner. Any road, why've you gone soft on old Nazi Reicker all of a sudden? It'd have been a good thing if they had shot him!"

Sean jumped to his feet. "You're daft in the head, you are. You don't know anything, Martin Bradan!"

"You don't know anything, Martin Bradan," Martin mimicked, mocking, wriggling his shoulders.

It was as if the tension of the storm had come back, like the spark which had struck between their sleeves on the Clough.

Sean shoved his hands in his pockets and strode off, squelching across the yard.

"Hey!" Martin shouted, running after him. "Where are you going?"

Charlie Bradan appeared at the gate. "Now then, you two, where are you off?"

"Nowhere, Dad," Martin muttered, scowling at the steaming ground.

Charlie Bradan eyed them over. "Then how about giving us a hand with that wall in Tupper's field? Sheep were in again this morning."

"Ah Dad..."

"Sean?"

"I've got to go," Sean said, his bones still heavy with anger.

Martin glared at him.

"In that case you haven't any excuse, have you, son? See you later, Sean."

As Martin slouched along behind his father, Sean heard Charlie Bradan say, "What was all that about?"

"Nothing."

"It's not like you and Sean to fall out."

"It blooming well is this summer!"

Sean did not wait to hear any more. He climbed the stone steps over the wall and set off at a fast walk, without looking back.

He climbed steadily, with rough fierce strides, slipping sometimes on the wet turf. The bracken stank rich and sour. High above him the wet screes of the Clough shone grey-black like gun-metal. He pulled off his T-shirt and stood a moment, his head thrown back, eyes closed to the sun, feeling the coolness of evaporating sweat on his back and neck. Martin was right – something was wrong with this summer.

Down below him he could see the tiny figures of Martin and his dad crossing Tupper's field, and Blackie and the colt. They looked like toy figures in a toy farm.

He stamped on. Flies buzzed at his back. Soon he was skirting the boulder field. He stayed under the screes – making for Clough Head. At some wall or unmarked boundary he passed off Bradan's land and onto Clegg's. He swatted at the sweat and the flies dancing before his eyes.

Through the bracken he heard the cool clear gurgle of the mountain stream. Trampling his way through to its rocky edge, he threw himself down, plunging his arms into the stony water. The coldness made him yell as he dipped his face and shook his head, splashing the rocks with spray. Then he drank from his hands. Sheep watched him from higher up, with pale slotted eyes, their backs steaming smokily against the blue sky.

"Caah! Caah!" A carrion crow beat upwards on black wings towards the scree face, and then there was only the buzzing insect hum of silence on the Clough. A silence which seemed to grind small as the pebbles in the clear stream. There was something wrong with this summer – even without Mattie Fiddler – something kept getting in the way of everything he and Martin did.

He sat back on his heels, very still, staring into the glitter of the stream's surface, trying to work out why Martin had made him so angry. What had changed? If only the stream would stay still for a moment it seemed he might find the answer. Martin would be leaving school next Easter.

Sean had a picture of himself, next summer, sitting in the school hall with only the scratching of pens and the rustle of exam papers breaking the silence, while, from somewhere up the valley, would come the faint roar of a tractor and the scent of new-mown hay.

He left the stream, carrying this mood with him like a cloud of tormenting flies he could not shake off.

Now he was on an unfamiliar flank of the Clough. He had never come so far alone, and the rock formations above him were strange and dark against the brightness of the sky. This would be the last summer – next year they would be neighbours, not mates.

Then he caught the faint whiff of a new scent in the air – cigarette smoke. He stopped and rubbed his mouth with the back of his hot hand. A tiny plume of smoke floated up from behind a large boulder. Instantly, he thought of Mattie Fiddler, and the fellside seemed to darken, as if a cloud shadow had swept over it.

He knew he should hurry very quietly away. But he's not on the Clough any more, he told himself. This was real life – not one of Martin's films. Even so, quietly, and careful of loose stones, he crept back down the sheep track, ducking and running low, crouching from boulder to boulder, rustling through the bracken, until he flung himself down in the dry lee of a boulder, where sheep had worn a hollow, judging that from here he would be able to see whoever it was that sat in the shadow of the higher rock.

Cautiously, he elbowed forward and poked his head round. Clouds of midges rose up over his bare back.

It was Nazi Reicker. Sean let his breath out in a low huff of relief. Reicker was sitting with his back to the boulder, staring away over the valley, his stick across his legs, and although his shirt was loosely open on his chest, he wore thirty years of solitude round him like a heavy grey coat.

It was the first time Sean had ever really looked at Reicker – the plates of his bony balding skull, the blue scar creasing his cheek, his pale eyes fixed on the middle distance in a solitary glare. He was hunched against the rock, and a rock's strength was in his broad shoulders and neck. Cigarette smoke curled from his thin lips as he ground out the dog-end on a stone. They called him Old Reicker, but really he was more weather-beaten than old.

The longer he spied on the man, the harder it was to get up and reveal himself. It was hard now to imagine Reicker singing in the darkness, with the little girl safe in his broad arms. It seemed like a dream. Reicker's face and the snapping jaws of the alsatian and the girl's legs dangling as she shrieked, and the men with rifles rushing in the darkness.

It was like an echo, Sean understood suddenly. He had seen an echo of something which had happened long ago, in the war, *as if he had seen it through Reicker's eyes...*

As he watched Reicker from his hiding place, he had the feeling that the old man was thinking about that moment also.

A horse-fly settled on Sean's cheek and, unthinkingly, he flicked at it with his hand. Reicker's gaze jerked towards him. Their eyes met. Guiltily, Sean jumped up and stepped out from behind the rock. "Hello," he blurted.

Nazi Reicker held him in his gaze, and Sean knew he had been recognised as one of the boys who stood on the pack-horse bridge roaring insults. He brushed fragments of bracken and soil off his bare chest and stomach.

"So," said Reicker.

Sean stared at the ground for a moment, as if he had been caught doing something wrong, wishing that somehow he could erase time, or the old man's memory of the things they had yelled. Then he looked up, "It was me," he said, "the other night with the police. I shouted. I thought they were going to shoot you – by accident."

Reicker said nothing. The sunlit turf was empty and still between them. Reicker picked up a tin flask from beside him, pulled out the stopper and sucked down three long gulps. The faintest shadow of an ironic smile flickered across Reicker's eyes. He looked down at the flask then thrust it towards Sean. "Here. Have some water."

Sean walked up the slope to him. "Thanks." He drank then wiped his mouth with the back of his fist. He could hardly bring himself to look at the old shepherd.

"Mr. Bradan says Emma is O.K. – well, she will be."

"What?"

"The little girl you found. She's O.K."

"Ah, yes." Reicker spoke with a strong accent.

Though he stood next to the man, the distance between them had not altered.

"They haven't caught Mattie Fiddler yet, though," Sean added. His words sounded empty in his own ears. Although this was all they had in common, it was like making an embarrassed conversation about the weather. And Reicker made no attempt to help him. He merely shrugged his big shoulders and reached for the flask again.

The scar on Reicker's weathered cheek crawled and rippled as he drank.

Sean pointed, "Did you get that in the war?"

Reicker's eyes swivelled to him. There was something in his look that made Sean want to leap up and run away – something hard, bitter, and thirty years in the making.

"I didn't mean . . ." he muttered.

"No," said Reicker, thumping the stopper back into the flask. He jerked his thumb at his cheek. "Six, seven years maybe after war. A fight. Yes? Fight? In the Hares and Dogs."

"The Hare and Hounds?"

"Yes." Reicker did not look away. His gaze stayed unrelentingly on Sean. "So. Now you know."

A great dark anvil of cloud was rearing up over Stang Head across the valley. Another storm. The light of the late afternoon was altering, coming low and unnaturally bright, splintered in the storm's shadow.

73

Sean wished he was back at Bradan's, that he had never come so far. He did not know what to say to Reicker. He guessed that the fight had been about the war, and, most probably, it would not have been a fair one.

With swift black energy the shadows of the clouds began to skim up the fell. The air cooled. The background hum of insects seemed to grow louder, until the bracken fizzed with it. Then, although the cloud seemed still to be on the far side of the valley, and they were still in sunlight, big splattering drops of rain began to fall. They both looked at the sky. Sean pulled on his damp T-shirt, as a jag of lightning danced off Stang Head, followed shortly by the almost subterranean rumble of thunder.

Reicker got to his feet. Sean beside him.

"Come," Reicker said. "Come, come." It sounded like 'kom' the way he said it. He strode off up the steep slope, pointing with his stick. "Here. Up here. An old mine for shelter. Yes."

It was as if the rain was following a step behind them. It spattered on their shoulders and yet the sunlight and the air lay before them. Just as they saw the gaping hole of an old mine tunnel it caught up and they ran. The raindrops were as hard as hail, stinging and blinding. They lurched into the mouth of the shaft as the fell vanished in the torrent of the storm. The air in the shaft was dank and chilly, ferny and dripping with age.

Panting, they both propped themselves against the rocky sides, as lightning jigged and hopped across the valley, closer and closer, until there was barely a gap for counting the thunder-miles across.

Blitzkrieg, thought Sean. The word just came into his head. Blitzkrieg. Lightning-war.

5

THERE WAS AN explosion over their heads. It reverberated round Stang, Clough, and Calder Knot, booming in the cauldron of the valley. Blue flashes lit Reicker's face, and Sean saw the big muscle twitching from the corner of his jaw to his brow, making the deep scar jerk and ripple.

Blitzkrieg. And as he watched the lightning flash on Nazi Reicker's face, he heard the drone of planes, the scream of shells, the 'chun-chun-chun' of anti-aircraft fire. He saw men running, crouched low in bursts of battle-light, and saw the sky criss-crossed by searchlights. And he saw a black line of men shuffling forward, queues stretching away into the darkness, and in the blue flashes swathes of them fell, but always the gap closed and the centipede crawled on over the stained sand. Boats were burning on an inky sea. Stukas shrieked, spitting fire, like metal hawks. And beneath the booms and cries, the shouts and explosions, there was silence. Unreal. Like an echo of a shout where no echo should be. And then there was a man running in this silence, a black silhouette, and four huge wolfish dogs were gaining on him...

Sean blinked, shook his head. Then there was only the waterfall over the mouth of the mine entrance, and the dim outline of familiar fells in the heavy steady rain. The trickle and gurgle of streams and gullies, and the low rumble of thunder many many miles away. Somewhere in the sodden bracken a black-faced ewe was bleating for her half-grown lamb.

Reicker lowered himself down and began to roll the thinnest of cigarettes, waiting patiently for the rain to cease. The blue smoke coiled and layered across the mouth of the shaft.

Pictures from comics, photographs in text books, clips of old newsreel, documentary, had flashed on an old man's face, etched in summer lightning. Sean could not take his eyes from him. Dunkirk had reverberated round the valley. The German victory of Dunkirk, and the smug squat tanks, crouched like toads, as Allied soldiers drowned. For the first time Sean understood that it had been a real thing, and forty years of Nazi Reicker's shunned sólitude had brought it to the Clough.

He turned away from the dripping cave entrance and from the smoke which hung in fine blue layers above Reicker's unyielding face, and let his gaze move to the darker recesses of the worked-out shaft, where older memories had made their dank and rock-bound peace. At last his eyes, growing accustomed to the darkness, rested on the shotgun where it lay by a black puddle. Old things gone and done. Perhaps that was why people hated Reicker, or feared him, because he stayed to remind them of a time when, for him and them, the war was not yet won.

And then, suddenly, he saw what he was looking at. A gun. "Reicker!" he gasped.

"Yes?"

"Look..."

Reicker glanced into the dark tunnel. "What?"

"A gun. There's a gun!"

Reicker stood, with the slackening rain like a grey web behind him. He lifted his chin. He peered. And then he looked at Sean, and his eyes said, Be silent. Listen. Don't move. Not a murmur. Slowly, slowly, he walked into the darkness, his cigarette still glowing in the cave mouth where he had dropped it. Slowly, slowly, Nazi Reicker bent, then snatched the gun up. And no sound came out of the dripping blackness save the smallest crack of the man's knees as he straightened.

As the rain outside began to stop, the sounds in the shaft seemed louder. The dripping of water onto rocks and into pools, a kind of breathy murmur of cold air in the darkness beyond. Neither of them moved. Then they heard a soft, sliding sound, something with weight to it, like the sound of a man shifting his shoulder against the cavern wall. Then a splash and the munch of wet shale under a shoe. Reicker's face looked all bones. He adjusted his grip on the shotgun – it became a weapon in his hands – as they saw the first faint pale smudge of Mattie Fiddler's face in the gloom.

He had been crouched behind them all the time.

Everything began to happen in slow motion.

"Run," Reicker hissed, pushing Sean back towards the entrance. "To Clegg's. Tell the police, boy. Run like death!"

And Sean ran, and slipped and fell and skidded down the wet side of the Clough, scissor-legged, his mind gone red with the pumping of his own blood, his chest cracking for breath. He scrabbled over a wall, knocking off stones, banging shins and elbows, and dropped on all fours onto a track which the storm had made into a waterfall. Soaked through, he hauled himself to his feet, and suddenly knew he was lost. The track forked steeply over the next rise and he could see no farm. He tried to grab a lungful of breath, then he dashed on, blindly, down the right hand fork, with the knowledge that if he had taken the wrong turn there would be nothing at all until he reached Clough Bottom, or stepped off the edge of the world. With the knowledge that Reicker's life might depend upon him being right.

Then he caught a jogging glimpse of a slate roof. The track dipped and he lost it, then rose, and he saw it again. The clutter of farm buildings shining clean and grey in the after-brilliance of the storm.

"Mr Clegg! Mr Clegg! Mr Clegg!" he began to shout, but he hadn't the breath to shout and run.

Yanking himself over the gate, his arms clicking, wrenched in their sockets, he stumbled on passed the back wall of the barn and into the empty farmyard.

He banged on the front door with both his fists, then leaned his forehead against the cool damp wood, snorting for breath. But no one came. He banged again. And again. And still no one answered. He tried the door but it was locked.

The pale smudge of Mattie Fiddler's face swam like a white dot before his eyes, as he dragged himself round to the back door. And that was locked too.

He had never been so alone in his life. "Mr Clee-eeeggg!" he yelled. But only the Clough echoed back to him.

Through the window he could see the empty kitchen, tea-leaves in the white sink, a newspaper on the table. He could read three words in the headlines – LOCAL MAN MURDERS.

In slow motion, he looked at the ground beneath his feet, until his eyes chose the thing he needed. A large stone. He picked it up with a grunt and crashed it against the window. The glass shattered, filling the sink. He bashed in the jagged edges, but still sharp teeth of glass stuck up and he dared not put his hands on them to pull himself through.

He pulled off his T-shirt to make a pad over the glass, then jumped and hauled himself through the broken window. Something scratched his shoulder, but he was in. Glass crunched under his shoes. The kitchen smelled empty. The house was silent, but through the hallway door he could see the black phone.

9. His fingers found the hole. 9. 9. "Reicker!" he yelled, when the voice answered. "He's got Mattie Fiddler. They're in the shaft! Please come. Please come!"

"Please try and keep calm," said the metallic voice in his ears. "Where are you calling from?"

"Clegg's Farm, near Clough Head. I've broken the window to get in."

"And what is your name?"

The voice seemed profoundly, ridiculously calm.

"Sean!" he yelled. "I was with Nazi Reicker on the Clough. In the storm. We sheltered in the mine. Then we found the gun. And then Mattie Fiddler was in the back. Reicker told me to run. Please, please Come!"

"We're on our way, Sean. Stay exactly where you are."

But it was not the police who arrived first, as Sean sat in the cool hallway, with his face in his hands. When he had put down the phone he had begun to shake uncontrollably. Hours seemed to pass. He was just about to give in to the urge to ring again when a key clicked in the front door.

Mr. Clegg was towering over him. "What the bloody hell...!" His gaze took in the scene through the kitchen door. Glass everywhere and blood on Sean's back. And before Sean could say anything, Clegg had hauled him to his feet. "Why you young hooligan! Breaking in, were you! By heck, lad, I'll show you..." Clegg's face was scalding red.

"No " Sean cried. "It's Reicker! Mr Clegg. I wasn't breaking in!" The man was about to hit him. But he held his fist
back.

"What about Reicker?" Clegg shook him. "I've had
enough bloody windows broken for him!"

"I had to break in! To phone the police. Reicker's got Mattie
Fiddler on the Clough. He told me to come. Honest, Mr Clegg!
Honest!" He was so exhausted that he almost fell when Clegg let
him go. And Clegg believed him. He had to, because police cars
were slamming like bullets into the farmyard.

Greeny was there, and the marksmen, but all in broad
daylight now. Sean stumbled his way through what had
happened one more time. "I'll show you where," he finished.

But Clegg said, "I know that shaft. There's only one on
my land. Biggest of the lot. Tourists go up to see it, like, so I
don't bother to fence it. I can show you."

"Right," said the Chief. "Well done, lad. You stay put.
Greenhall, stay here with him – have a look at that shoulder.
Come on!"

And the farmhouse was empty again, save for Sean and old
Greeny.

"Let's get you cleaned up, lad," Greeny said. "That's a
nasty gash. Wouldn't surprise me if you didn't need a stitch
in that."

He sat Sean down on a kitchen chair. "Perhaps I'd better
have someone take you to the hospital."

Sean could not feel anything, except for a warmish tickle
trickling between his shoulder blades. "It doesn't hurt. Let
me stay until Reicker's safe down."

Greeny nodded. He put a towel on Sean's shoulders, then
set about making a pot of tea. He even swept up the glass and
put it in the bin. It seemed odd, even at that moment, to see
the police officer with a brush and dustpan in his hands, as if
he had broken a plate.

Sean drank the sweet tea and felt a bit better. From time to
time the radio in Greeny's pocket crackled and chattered.

"What were you doing with old Nazi Reicker then?" said
Greeny. "Tormenting him as usual?"

Sean shook his head.

"And where's your partner in crime – young Martin Bradan, today?"

Sean shook his head again.

Greeny's face changed. The hardness went out of it. "Listen Sean, you did right. Tell you what, I'll have them fetch your dad."

It was almost dark by the time the police came down off the Clough. Dad stood for an age with his hand resting lightly on Sean's arm. He had put his jacket round him, when he had seen how much Sean was shivering not caring that it would get blood on it.

A calm pink sunset was glowing over Calder Knot, the sky washed clean by the storms. The windscreens of the police cars shone pink in the light where they were parked among the barns and the old bath tubs which served as water troughs in Clegg's yard.

From time to time, Greeny gave them a progress report. Reicker was O.K. Mattie Fiddler had come without protest. In fact, he was crying. The police were having to help him down the Clough because he was in such a state he could hardly walk.

From time to time, Sean looked up at his dad. And his dad looked back, his face gentle and stern. Once he said, "I'm glad you had the courage to break the window, Sean."

"It wasn't courage. I was scared to death. It was the only thing to do."

Dad smiled a half smile. "Same difference. That's what people get medals for."

Sean looked away, out of the open door, into the stillness and calm of the sun going down.

At last, they saw the knot of officers coming down the steep slope. Sean and his dad stood in the doorway, watching.

They led Mattie Fiddler to a car. He was handcuffed between two policemen – a pale thing between their dark uniforms. His shirt was torn, his head lolled and flopped on his chest. He looked more like an elderly invalid than a murderer. More like an old, ill man being helped by two male nurses. They bundled him into the back seat.

Reicker was following behind, hunched and silent and grey. Two of the officers stopped and waited for him, as he walked slowly but steadily into the farmyard.

Sean went to meet him. "I'm glad you're O.K.," he said.

The distance was still between them in the fading light. Uncrossable.

Reicker nodded. "Yes. O.K. Thank you. For running – thank you." He held out his hard veined hand.

Sean shook it. Frowning, he said, "Those things we shouted... I... We... it was stupid. I mean..."

"Nazi?" said Reicker. He glanced over Sean's head at the two police officers who were waiting. He shrugged. "When I was your age, I was."

The Egg-Man

For my Mum

"Jane Black
  On her back
  In the long grass
  Doing that!
  Jane Black
  Got the sack
  Was seen in the long grass
  Doing that!"
The girls chanted.
  "One, Two
  It isn't true!" Jane sang back and hopped out of the
turning rope. She dashed round to the end of the queue as
Bridget Hennessy took the rope on the next skip.
  "Bridget Black
  On her back
  In the long grass
  Doing that!"
Bridget began to giggle so much she stepped on the rope
and almost tripped over.
  "Come on, girls," called Mrs Jackson. "It's time you were
all at home. I want to lock these gates."
  Bridget only giggled louder. Jane pressed her hand over
her mouth and laughter spurted between her fingers. They
never sang that skipping song when teachers were about. No
one had noticed Mrs Jackson walk past them. The seven girls
ran out of the school gate and Mrs Jackson swung it closed,
shutting in the empty playground for the weekend.

"Bye!"
"Bye!"
"See you on Monday!" Their calls scattered sparrows off the pavement.

Bridget and Jane walked together. Bridget was still laughing. "That song's rude!" she snorted, and her face went red, until she begun to cough.

Jane thumped her on the back. "Daft bat! Shut up, Bridget! Let's go down Back Lane and over the field." Without waiting for an answer, she hared across the road, Bridget chasing after her.

Back Lane was not really back of anything, apart from a few scruffy fields and hawthorn hedges which separated the edge of the town from the industrial estate and the council houses. Sometimes gipsy horses grazed the fields – black and white ponies that were too wild to get close to. The only house on Back Lane was the egg-man's, surrounded by ramshackle outbuildings, twisted grey apple trees, and bits of scrap. The house itself was grey, with four blind dusty windows. It did not look lived in and nobody went there.

As they passed it, Bridget stopped. "Go and knock on the door – I dare you."

"You do it," Jane said.

"I dared you first! Go on. You have to."

Jane looked at the house. There were torn lace curtains in the bottom windows. Brown paint was peeling off the front door, and the garden was tall with weeds, still brittle and dry from the winter. A rusty bed-stead was propped against the wall and a few hens pecked and scratched beneath it. No one went near the egg-man. He was mental. Everyone was scared of him.

Bridget had stopped laughing. "Go on, then." She gave Jane a little shove, then crouched by the gate-post of the field, so she could watch.

The egg-man had poisoned his wife, and Robert Gates said he had seen the egg-man chop off a hen's head with an axe, and the hen had kept running round and round with the blood coming out of its neck.

Jane glanced helplessly at Bridget, but Bridget only flapped her hand impatiently and pulled a face, so that she had no choice but to run up the path, brambles whipping at her bare legs. She banged three times on the door, then fled back along the path and dropped down by Bridget. For a moment nothing happened. Then the door creaked open.

"Is that you, Nellen?" The egg-man's head appeared around the door. He had a thin beaky face, grey as dust. On his nose he wore a pair of National Health spectacles, mended at the edge with a bit of sticking-plaster.

"Oh look," Bridget hissed, as the egg-man stepped outside. Her face began to go red with suppressed giggles. "He's wearing his pyjama top over his shirt!"

"Nelly?" The egg-man peered round his scruffy garden, moving his head in little scraggy jerks. "Is that you, dear?"

"Who's Nelly?" Jane whispered.

"His wife, what he murdered," Bridget whispered back.

Jane tugged at Bridget's cardigan sleeve. "Come on away. Let's go. I don't like it. . . " She did not want to see any more of the egg-man, with his broken spectacles and his claw-like hands.

"Scaredy-cat, scaredy-cat!" sang Bridget under her breath.

Now the front door closed and, once more the house stared blank and blind across the bare fields.

"Come on away," Jane said again, beginning to get to her feet. But Bridget tugged her back down.

"Go and knock again."

"No!" Jane shook her head fiercely.

"Well, I'll go then, scaredy-cat. We can pretend to be his wife come back to haunt him." Bridget's eyes were brown and bright. The ribbon was sliding out of her black hair. She could never keep ribbons tied.

"I've got to go home," Jane muttered. "I'm late. My mam'll be waiting."

But Bridget was already creeping across the lane, keeping low behind the wall. Her thin white legs stuck out of the wrinkles of her grey socks. She banged loudly on the door, then scrambled back to the gate post, clutching at Jane's arm.

The egg-man's face appeared above the tatty lace curtains. A moment later the door opened again, and he stood there, his thin lips pressed together. "Nelly?"

They saw his mouth move in a whisper. More than ever Jane wanted to run away.

Bridget cupped her hands round her lips. "It is I," she quavered, in a low ghostly voice. "I have returned to see you, my dearest." Her voice cracked. She stuffed her fist into her mouth and clutched Jane tighter, shaking with silent laughter.

Jane watched the egg-man. He was standing quite still, staring at the ground. Then he turned slowly, his shoulders hunched, and shuffled back into the house.

She did not wait for Bridget, but quickly climbed over the gate and began to run across the field. A mist was rising from the ditches and hollows and the sun was going down behind the gasworks. Her long black shadow ran beside her, skimming the thistles.

Bridget caught up. "I have returned to see yoo-ooo!" she hooted like an owl, making her eyes round and staring in her thin face.

"I am the ghost of Nelly Black
   Dead in the long grass
   On my back!"

Jane began to laugh. "You're daft in the head, Bridget Hennessy! What if he'd caught us?"

But Bridget only skipped and twizzled ahead of her, crying,

"Ha-ha-ha! Hee-hee-hee!
   Try if you can
   You can't catch me!"

But Jane did, and they staggered, panting and laughing to the gap in the hawthorn hedge which was their short-cut home. "I wonder what her real surname was? You know, his name. Then we could be really scarey."

"I don't know," said Jane. "Ouch!" The hedge had grabbed hold of her long hair, and she had to crouch patiently as Bridget untangled her.

"I'll ask my mam," said Jane when she was free.

Bridget looked at her thoughtfully. "Perhaps we could get a real ghost from the churchyard..."

"Don't be silly. There aren't such things as real ghosts anyway."

"Yes there are," said Bridget. "In fact, there's one behind yoo-ooo!"

Jane did not fall for that. But it was almost dark now, and she still had to walk down her street alone. "Give over, Bridget. Are you coming out after tea?"

"No, I can't tonight. Mam wants me in the shop – I'll give you some free chips if you come."

"See you tomorrow anyhow. Tarra!"

"Bye!"

"Get those mucky clod-hoppers off my clean floor!"

"Sorry, Mam. We came over the back field." Jane knelt to untie the knot in her shoe-lace.

Mum watched her, hands on hips. "I wondered where you'd got to. And I've told you before about those fields. It's not safe for a young lass to take short cuts these days."

"I was with Bridget. Anyway, nobody ever goes there."

"Well, come on. Hurry up. Your dad's waiting for his tea."

"Hello, poppet," said Dad when she went into the living-room. "You in trouble again?" Then he called through to Mum, "What's for breakfast?" That was his joke when he was on night-shifts. He had only just got up, and there was a scrap of paper stuck on his chin where he had cut himself shaving.

"Hotpot," Mum called back. "Come and get it before it goes cold."

"Hotpot! For breakfast! Whatever will the woman think of next!" said Dad and winked at Jane.

"It's May Day on Monday," Mum said, as she cut the loaf into doorsteps. A secret look passed between Jane and Dad. May the first was Mum's birthday, and they had almost finished making her present.

"And we finish school in another week," Jane said. "A whole week for half-term..."

"Holiday for some," said Mum. "Means work for others."
Mum was always like this when Dad was on nights. She
could not sleep well without him beside her, and brown
shadows appeared under her eyes.

"Never mind," said Dad. "Only another week for me as
well, and I'll be off nights. Right glad I'll be too. It's worse
this time of year. I go to bed in the dark and get up in the
dark, almost. It's like living in a tunnel."

When tea was finished, Jane and Dad hurried upstairs.

"What about this washing up?" Mum yelled after them.

"I don't keep a dog and bark as well!" Dad shouted down.
"Eh up!" he whispered. "That'll make her mad!"

They went into the big bedroom and Dad locked the door.
Jane pulled the sheets and blankets straight on her Mum and
Dad's bed, then got the box from underneath.

"I said," said Mum, knocking loudly on the door "what
about this, washing-up?"

"I'll do it after, Mam. Go away."

"Don't you tell me to go away, miss!"

"You can't come in," Dad said, grinning at Jane.

"And we've left the key in the door so you can't spy
neither."

"Oh, can't I now," said Mum. They could tell by her voice
that she was only pretending to be cross. Suddenly the key
fell out of the keyhole, and the end of a hair-grip wriggled
through.

Jane yelled, ran to the door and clapped her hands over the
keyhole, but Mum was already going back downstairs,
singing to herself.

"She's dying to see what it is," Dad said, unfolding the
tissue paper from the picture. He laid it gently on the bed. It
looked like a painting made from jewels, glowing and
shimmering softly. And it had taken since Christmas to
make.

Jane gently brushed her fingers over the surface. It was
softer than velvet because the picture was made of feathers,
hundreds of them, all carefully glued and over-lapped. The
eyes of her mother looked up at her from the portrait, soft

and bright as a mallard's neck. It was the most beautiful thing she had ever seen, and she had helped to make it.

"Come on, Jane," said Dad softly. "Get the glue. We've still got the rest of her hair to do, and the background. We'll have to hurry if we want it finished in time."

They placed the box of feathers on the bed, and Dad began to select them and cut them with the edge of a razor-blade. It was Jane's job to hold them in place on the picture until the glue set. There were only a few feathers left in the box now – pigeons' feathers and pheasants', seagulls' and canaries', and a few bits of the peacock feathers which they had used to make the neck of Mum's dress where it showed.

Dad frowned. "What we could really do with is a dead spadger," he said. "There's hardly enough here to finish her hair. We need some more browns, little soft browns. You'll have to see what you can find tomorrow, otherwise we'll be in dead-lumber."

"I'll do my best," said Jane.

"And we could do with something with a bit of colour in it, just to liven up the background. Here, put your finger on that – and careful not to shift it, mind."

Jane pressed the tiny feather down, gently, as he had shown her how.

"You could win a prize with this, Dad. I bet you could win a hundred pounds."

Dad smiled and shook his head. "Not with this one, lass. This is for her, and the best prize will be the look on her face when she sees it." He was silent while he concentrated on cutting a sliver of fine white down from a goose feather to make a highlight in her hair.

Jane picked up the mahogany frame that would go round the picture when it was finished. Dad had made that as well, and he had written *Mavis* in gold letters in the bottom left-hand corner. Mavis was Mum's name, and it meant 'song-thrush'.

Dad put a tiny dab of glue on the card, then placed the white on it. Jane could see his fingers shaking with carefulness as he gently guided it into place with the tip of his nail.

"Gently," he said. "Mind you don't blow it away."

Jane held it down. She had learnt not to press too hard, or the glue came through the feather and stuck to your finger, then, when you lifted your hand, you pulled the feather away as well. If you didn't press enough the feather would not stick properly.

"Eh, damnation!" said Dad, searching through the few remaining feathers.

"Don't swear," Jane said.

"Pardon me, your ladyship! But we've run out of spadgers and thrushes, and all we've got left is a few mangy blackbirds, canaries and squabs. All we can do is a bit of the background until we find some more."

"We've got some starlings," Jane said. "But they're a bit scraggy."

Dad folded his arms and chewed his bottom lip. "What's in the pillow on your bed?"

Jane shook her head. "Just foam. You used all the feather pillows when you did that owl for the show."

"Oh, aye. So I did. And it only won second prize at that."

"Only because Arthur Wallace cheated and bought all those parrot feathers from the zoo!" Jane said hotly.

"Too true," Dad agreed. "That blooming parrot of his wasn't a picture – it was taxidermy. He should have been disqualified!"

Dad's owl had been made from feathers out of their best pillows, and it had held a white mouse in its claws. But Arthur Wallace, who had won first prize, had done a parrot from parrots' feathers, which didn't seem right, although Mrs Mayor had said it was "Oh, such artistry," when she gave him the red rosette.

From downstairs came the slow formal chime of the wall clock.

"Heck!" Dad began to gather up the boxes. "I'll be late for work. Quick, wrap it up, Jane."

They put everything back into the box and hid it under the bed again, locked in Dad's old suitcase.

92

Then he grabbed his jacket from the back of the chair and unlocked the bedroom door.

"Hold on," said Jane. "You've still got paper on your chin."

"Ta. Now listen, tomorrow you hunt high and low. We've only got two days left. Get that Bridget to help you. Night-night!"

He clattered down the stairs, kissed Mum as she sat in her chair, then slammed out of the front door into the dark street.

Mum stared after him.

Jane said from the foot of the stairs "I'll do the washing up now."

"No need, love," said Mum. "It's done."

Jane studied Mum's hair where the lamplight fell on it. There were shining glints. That bit of white Dad had put in was just right.

"What are you gawping at?" Mum said.

"The cat's mother!" Jane cried, and fled upstairs as Mum chased her.

2

IT WASN'T until next morning that Jane remembered the egg-man.

"Mum?" she said, as she helped peg out the washing in the back yard.

"Whaf?" said Mum, between the pegs in her mouth.

"You know the egg-man on Back Lane. What's his real name?"

"Ifia Blaf," Mum spluttered. She took another peg from between her teeth and pegged on a pair of Jane's school socks.

"What?" said Jane.

Mum took the rest of the pegs from between her teeth. "Isaiah Black. Why?"

"Bridget asked."

"Did she now?"

Jane suddenly remembered Bridget chanting,

"I am the ghost of Nelly Black
Dead in the long grass
On my back!"

and she began to laugh. "He's not *really* called Black, is he, Mam?"

"Yes. What's so funny about that?"

But Jane only laughed harder until the wind blew a wet sheet across her face. Then Mum began to laugh as well as she fought her way out, like a daft white ghost.

"Shusssh!" Mum hissed, pointing to the upstairs window. Dad was asleep.

Quietly, they hung out the rest of the washing, and the sheets and shirts snapped and flapped in the bright April wind.

"Right. You can go now. But I want you in for tea-time, mind."

"I will be. Can I take two apples?"

"Yes. And there's some money on the sideboard for chips."

"Ta, Mam."

Jane ran down the street and met Bridget running in the opposite direction.

"Feathers," said Jane.

"Oh no!" said Bridget, clapping her hand to her forehead. "Not again!"

"Please," said Jane. "It's important."

Bridget yanked her ribbon into a knot. "Oh, alright. The fields are best – unless we go into town and see what we can get on the market."

Jane shook her head. "Mum doesn't like me going into town."

"Right then," said Bridget. "Fields."

They ran down the alley by Bridget's mum and dad's 'Superior Fish and Chips' and squeezed through the wooden fence posts. They came out into the field behind the gas-works.

"Hey!" said Jane, remembering. "I'll tell you what the egg-man's called, but you've got to say 'why' after I say his name."

Bridget looked puzzled. "Alright."

"The egg-man is called Isaiah."

"Why?"

"Because one eye's higher than the other!" Before Bridget could clout her she skipped away.

Bridget groaned loudly, then caught up.

"But listen to this – really, truly, he's called Isaiah Black. And so she *was* called Nelly Black!"

To her surprise, Bridget did not laugh. Instead she stopped still amongst the thistles. "That's weird," she said. Bridget's Mum was Irish and knew all about ghosts. Bridget's Mum often said that things never happened by coincidence.

Jane stood still, looking at Bridget's thin white face. "Yes. It is a bit." Then she grinned. "I am the ghost of Nelly Black, and I have returned to haunt yoo-ooo!" She lifted her arms and ran at Bridget.

Bridget yelled and dashed off.

"It's still weird," said Bridget, when she caught up. "Anyhow, what kind of feathers does your dad want now?"

"Anything. But a dead spadger would be best."

"Yack!" said Bridget, pulling a face. "I'm not picking up a maggoty sparrow just for your dad to win a prize."

"It isn't for a prize. It's for Mum's birthday. Oh Bridget, it's beautiful. You'll see."

They began to hunt about. The cold bright wind blew their hair across their faces and flicked up the hems of their skirts.

Jane found the first feather. "Rook," she said. It was speared into the soft ground like an arrow. Gently, she plucked it out and stroked her finger up the blue-black gleam of it.

Then Bridget found a muddy seagull's feather floating in a puddle.

"Do you want it?"

"I suppose so." Jane looked uncertain. But she took it anyway.

"Let's try by the hedge," said Bridget. "There might be nests there."

They walked slowly by the hawthorn hedge. Its black tangle was misted with green buds. But there were no nests and no feathers. And by lunch-time they had still only found two.

They sat on the wooden gate which led into Back Lane, eating Jane's apples. A magpie laughed and flicked its tail at them as it flew over the scruffy field. Behind them was the egg-man's orchard and further down the lane was his house and the gate they had hidden behind.

Bridget munched at her apple-core, but Jane stared miserably at the two feathers in her left hand. They just *had* to find some more. These two weren't much good anyway, because they needed brown feathers, not black or white ones.

A rooster crowed in the egg-man's orchard. Hens clucked and burred as they scratched in the mud. Somewhere among the tumbled outbuildings there was a pond where a drake shook his wings and laughed like an idiot, "Waa-ck-wack-wack-wack!"

"Come on," said Jane suddenly, and jumped from the gate into the lane.

"Oh no," said Bridget, shaking her head.

"But there'll be lots of feathers."

"I'm not going in there," said Bridget.

"Scaredy-cat," Jane said, uncertainly.

"He might be hiding behind a tree with an axe," Bridget said, staring at the grey twisted boughs of the orchard. "In his pyjamas," she added in a whisper.

Jane lost her courage. She stood by the gate again. The wind blew Bridget's skirt up from her white knees. They both looked down the lane to the grey house where no one ever called.

"But it's Saturday," Jane said, guessing. "He'll have gone up town to sell his eggs on the market."

Bridget slid off the gate and stood beside her. "I suppose we could just look in the lane . . ."

So they did. Nervously, they peered under the hedges and

into the damp ditch where yellow celandines and stinging-nettles were growing thick and tangled. And at last they found feathers – the small brown pillow feathers of hens, and a whole wing torn from a carcase by a fox or a cat. It was on the far bank of the ditch. Bridget poked to reach it with a stick, turning her face away because the smell of the dead hen was in the hedge. But the stick knocked the wing into the slime-green water, and neither of them fancied getting it out.

Now they were almost at the garden wall. Jane crouched to pick up a white duck feather, soft, yet stiff as a starched sheet.

"Oh, look," Bridget pointed through the gap where the hedge and the wall met. "A kitten! We could catch it – for a pet."

"Don't be daft," said Jane. The kitten disappeared round the side of the house.

"Oh come on," said Bridget, stuffing her feathers into her cardigan pocket. "Let's go and look. He isn't here."

"How do you know?"

"I just know. I'm like my mam. I just *know* some things."

Jane knew Bridget was lying. The egg-man probably *had* gone to his stall on the market, but all Bridget wanted was to hold a warm soft kitten in her cold hands. Before she could stop her, Bridget was scrambling and squeezing through the gap, and her red ribbon was left caught in the dark thorns of the hedge.

"Bridget! Bridget!" Jane whispered, but in her head she was shouting. Bridget had vanished. The wind rattled a loose sheet of corrugated iron on the roof of a shed. 'Nick-nock-nick-nock,' like a tapping wooden hammer the door of a hutch slammed and opened and bits of old straw blew away. She picked her way through the mud and the hens scattered this way and that. A rooster stood proud on a rusty iron bath-tub and crowed at her.

"Bridget? Where are you?"

"Behind yooo-oo!" quavered Bridget's voice.

Jane swung round. But no one was there. Empty doorways gaped, planks hung askew and an old sign, crooked on its pole, creaked as if about to drop from the rusty nail. She was afraid now. It was only Bridget being daft, but she was afraid. "Bridget, give over. Where are you?"

"Dead and buried in me grave," the voice quavered over her shoulder.

"Bridget!" Jane turned. But there was no sign of her friend anywhere.

"I'm going home," Jane said louder, and pretended to walk off towards the gate and the house.

"Come on Jane. I was only kidding." Bridget stepped out from a shed, wisps of straw stuck in her cardigan and a streak of mud on her cheek.

"That was stupid. What if he'd got you?" Jane's face felt tight. Her heart was banging against her ribs.

"Well, he never. Anyway, it was your idea to come." Bridget pressed her lips together, so her face was thin and white and bony. "It's you that wants the blooming feathers!" Then she smiled. "Come on, let's explore."

Cautiously, they made their way through the sheds and coops and stacks of wood, skirting muddy puddles. "If he comes," said Bridget, "you run for help, and I'll scream. I can scream louder than you."

"No you can't."

"Yes, I can!" Bridget opened her mouth, but Jane clapped her hand over the round red hole before the sound came out. They clung together for a moment, laughing.

"Let me go!" Bridget wriggled.

"Shusssh!" Jane pressed her finger to her lips. They crept round the corner of a shed, and the duck pond lay before them, brown and muddy. There were a few grubby white ducks, and the webby prints of their feet made a pattern at the pond's edge.

"Quack-quack-quack!" Bridget called, and the white drake answered her, clicking his yellow bill and waggling his tail. They began to throw handfuls of grass onto the water, pretending they were breadcrumbs. But the ducks would not come to them.

"Don't forget to pick up feathers," Jane said. The egg-man's orchard did not seem so frightening now they were in it. Just dirty and scruffy. There were rusty buckets and broken jam jars green with slime, hidden in the long grass. Soon her hands and pockets were stuffed with brown, white, grey, even speckled feathers. She thought of what Dad would say when she showed them to him, and began to hum softly. Now, Mum's present could be finished in time.

But Bridget was off again. "Jane! Jane! There's that kitten!" she called and went chasing back amongst the sheds and hutches, scattering the hens and setting a commotion in the duck pond. Jane only had time to glimpse her red skirt and her black hair flying as she disappeared from view.

"Bridget!" she said, exasperated, and had no choice but to run after her.

Bridget was on her hands and knees by a pile of grey timbers. "Come on, pussy! Come on, little puss," she crooned. "I won't hurt you." She made a soft clicking sound with her tongue.

"Don't run off like that!" Jane knelt beside her. Two dark eyes, round as pennies, peered at her from the dark hollows amongst the planks. The kitten came closer. Its fur was almost orange. Bridget reached slowly towards it, but the little creature shot away, dashing from the wood pile towards the back of the house.

"If we catch it," Bridget gasped as they followed. "You could keep it at your house and I could bring fish from the shop."

"You can't just take it. It might be the egg-man's pet."

Bridget stopped. She gave Jane a long, scornful, disbelieving look. "Don't you know? He drowns cats in that pond!"

The kitten was cornered where the garden wall met the side of the house, by the back door. It arched its fluffy back and hissed at them.

"It's only frightened," Bridget said, "because it thinks we might be him. Come on, little pussy . . ." she crooned. "We'll save you."

But the kitten made a dash for the door, and disappeared

into the house. The back door was open, just a crack, and both Jane and Bridget froze when they saw the gap.

"He must be in . . ." Jane hissed. The feathers went sticky in her hand. They stayed still as stones, listening. The wind blew the door open wider. It creaked on its hinges.

"We've got to save it," Bridget gave Jane one desperate glance. "Else he'll drown it!"

Jane didn't know if Bridget was making it up about the egg-man drowning cats, but the look on Bridget's face convinced her. "We *can't* go in there!" she said.

Bridget pushed her hair from her face. She stood up. Jane stared at her. Then Bridget knocked. Each knock shoved the door wider. And nobody came. "It must have been the wind blew it open."

Jane went to the kitchen window. The glass was so dirty it was hard to see through, but she saw the kitten – a tawny blur on the floor.

She wished that they had never come. Nothing would stop Bridget now. And she couldn't just leave her. It was like a dream. Bridget opened the door and the smell of the house met them – musty and sour and stale. And in the dream they went into the egg-man's kitchen, where cardboard egg-trays were piled high on the table, and unwashed pans littered the sink. Through another door they could see the sitting-room, brown and dark, with yellow newspaper in the unlit fireplace, and texts in heavy brown frames on the wall. 'He Is Able To Succour Them That Are Tempted'. 'Who Teacheth Us More Than The Beasts Of The Earth, And Maketh Us Wiser Than The Fowls Of Heaven?'. The words were written in stern golden letters.

They stood in the doorway together, gazing at the dark dusty room. By a chair was a basket of sewing threads, and shirts to be mended. And on the arm of the chair was a shirt with a needle in it. The needle had been there so long it had gone rusty, and the brown stain of rust was spreading through the grey cotton. On a low round table, tea was set for two, though the silver tea-pot was brown with tarnish, and a dead moth lay in one of the china cups.

In the dream they walked into the room, where dust was like the silence settled over everything. "It's just as she left it..." said Jane, gazing down at the rusty needle, and the tiny delicate stitches gone yellow with age.

"I feel like a ghost..." said Bridget.

In a round heavy frame above the mantelpiece was a yellowing photograph. Nelly Black looked down at them from under a straw hat. One hand was gloved and the other bare. Her face was long and oval, and smiling coldly. At her shoulder stood a stern young man in a black suit. He had a thin face and a moustache, and his eyes frowned at the flowers in his wife's hat.

"That must be them when they got married."

Bridget nodded.

They went through another door into the hallway, and there was the same straw hat hanging on a peg, but the flowers had long since withered and shrivelled away. Beneath the hat hung a long grey coat. Jane touched it with her finger-tip and the grey came away leaving a streak of black satin.

They crept up the staircase and three doors opened off the landing. Through one they could see the bath, and through another a red dress draped over the end of a neatly made bed. And through the third they could see the tumble and mess of the egg-man's bedroom, with stained sheets hanging from the mattress and a shaving mug on the floor.

They went into Nelly Black's bedroom and though the dust lay thick on the white counterpane and dead leaves lay on the window-ledge, the room seemed bright and quiet and orderly, and the faded red dress was neatly folded although a spider had built a web across the collar.

Then Jane saw the primroses – not dead and faded, although the rest of the room was like a pressed flower, but yellow and bright in a small glass vase, their green leaves arranged around them. The small vase stood on the dressing-table, bright as the April day they had left. Fresh and alive, as if Nelly Black had picked them that morning. And, suddenly, she was no longer dreaming, but trespassing like a burglar. "Bridget! Come on!"

And Bridget woke too. She clutched Jane's sleeve. "Listen!"

A van was pulling up in the mud. She raced to the window. The egg-man was climbing from the driving-seat of the battered old vehicle. "Quick! He's back!" She grabbed Jane to pull her from the room, but they heard the back door close. They were trapped.

3

"I'LL MAKE us a nice pot of tea. There we are – a spoon for me, a spoon for you, and one for the pot." Through the floorboards they could hear him whispering. "You just rest your feet and I'll make us a nice pot of tea, Nell."

Jane and Bridget huddled behind the bed. His footsteps shuffled to the hallway, then back to the kitchen. They heard the clatter of cups, the rattle and slither of cutlery in a drawer.

"Who's he talking to?" Bridget murmured.

"Her," Jane breathed back. "We've got to get out of here." What if they had to hide all night? she thought. What if he found them? Beside her, Bridget was close to tears.

"It's all my fault," she whimpered.

"Hush," said Jane.

"Yes, my dear, we did very nicely today," they heard the egg-man say in a creaky whisper. His spoon rang on the cup as he stirred his tea. "I'll buy you that red dress from Whittackers, Nellen. We'll go to a show, eh? Tee-hee! We'll go to a show." Down below, in the dark dusty room, the egg-man began to sing,

"Ye zephyrs gay that fan the air
And wanton thro' the grove,
Oh whisper to my charming fair,
I die for her I love."

Jane pressed her hand to her mouth, biting her fingers, to stop herself crying out.

"Well, what do you say to that? Eh? If we go to a show at the Grand on Alfred Street, and you in a red dress, Nell? Eh?

Or we could go up Broadway to the Palace..." The old man sniggered and clucked and shuffled back to the kitchen. "Now then, Isaiah. Now then, you mustn't be forgetting the quackers and cluckers! Quackers and cluckers! Hee-hee! Oh, that was peachy, Nell. That was peachy! No, I'll not be forgetting them."

They heard the back door creak and bang closed, then the scrape of a pail in the backyard. His footsteps shuffled away.

"Quick! Come on!"

"What if he comes back?" Bridget stared up at Jane.

"Come on, Bridget!"

They crept downstairs. The kitten was sitting on the window ledge but neither of them had time for it now. The back door was closed. Very carefully Jane turned the handle and pulled. The hinges squealed. They peered through the gap and saw the egg-man among the sheds with his back to them, scattering grain to the hens which pecked and squabbled at his feet.

"Now," said Jane. They yanked the door open and fled round the side of the house, Jane still clutching her handful of feathers. The hedge dragged at them as they struggled through the gap into the lane, where long black shadows stretched in the late afternoon sunlight.

Quickly, they ran across the lane, clambered over the gate, and lay gasping in the long grass of the field. Safe.

"I thought he'd find us," Bridget said. "And lock us up in a shed!" Her hands and face were streaked with dust, her cardigan snagged and torn.

"He was talking to her as if she was there!" said Jane. "Just as if she was really there!"

"He's bonkers," Bridget agreed. Suddenly she pulled Jane down. The egg-man was across the lane, behind the hedge.

They stared at him from the long grass in the shadow of the five-barred gate.

"This lass so neat,
    with smiles so sweet,
  Has won my right good will...
  Te-tum-te-tum

103

Tee-tum-tee-tum

Sweet lass of Richmond Hill," he sang in his cracked voice. "Yes, we'll go to a show at the Grand, Nellen. . ." he muttered, and tears trickled from behind his spectacles and down his thin ugly face.

"Lovely," said Dad. "They're just the job. We should have enough to finish it with these. Now, you listen for the clock." He sorted the feathers into piles of different colours. Some of them were squeezed, their shafts broken, where Jane had clutched them hard in fright. "Your mam's just popped next door to help Alice choose material for new curtains – and you know what that means. It'll be 'Ooh, I saw a lovely bit of stuff, just right for our sitting-room,' when she gets back." He grinned at Jane. Then he frowned. "You're quiet tonight, poppet."

Jane sat on the edge of the bed, which was still warm from Dad so recently lying in it. She smoothed the sheet with her hand and shook her head.

"Not sickening, are you?"

"No, Dad."

"Well, come on then – you dab some glue on there, while I cut a bit of this, eh?"

Jane did as he asked, but although the picture was more beautiful than ever, her heart wasn't in it. She wanted to tell him about the red dress with the spider's web woven across the collar, about the moth in the china teacup, about the needle rusting away in the frayed shirt, and the egg-man talking to himself. But she could not – not without telling him how they had stolen into the egg-man's house and almost got caught. At last, she said, "Dad, have you ever seen someone singing and crying at the same time?"

Dad put down the feather and rubbed his chin, looking at her. "Well that's a teaser. . . Crying and singing? Hmmm. . . At funerals, yes, singing hymns and weeping – I've done that myself, at your Uncle David's funeral. Mind, you'd be too young to remember that." He considered Jane thoughtfully. "Crying and singing? What made you ask that, I wonder?"

"Nothing. Bridget and me saw a man, that's all."

"Oh, he was probably drunk. Don't you mind him."

Jane nodded, but the egg-man had not been drunk, she was certain.

Dad placed the feather on the glue, and said quietly, "This man – did he say anything? I mean, did he say anything to upset you?" He did not look at her as he waited for a reply.

"Oh no," said Jane quickly. "He never saw us."

"Well, that's alright then," Dad said, and smiled. "There's nowt as queer as folk – that's what your grandma always used to say. Mind you, I always reckon that most folk are harmless if you keep your distance and treat them right." He bent over his work, his broad blunt fingers delicate on the small feathers. They had almost finished the hair.

Jane picked up a quill and stroked the barbs down the wrong way, breaking open the feather.

"Hoy! We might need that," said Dad.

"Sorry. Dad?" she began, but the clock downstairs began to chime.

Hastily, they wrapped the picture and put everything out of sight.

"Jane?" Mum called up the stairs. "I'm back. Tell your dad to get up or he'll be late!"

"Cheeky madam," said Dad, and hurried off to his shift.

But Jane did not go down. Instead she stayed on her parents' bed, listening to the wind rattling through the street and watching her reflection on the black window-pane. And, all the while, she thought of the egg-man talking to himself in his dark dusty room, and singing, as tears dribbled from beneath his scratched spectacles, until his loneliness was like an ache in her throat.

After lunch on Sunday, Bridget came round. They went out into the backyard and Bridget began to play Two Ball against the wall, singing,

"One, two, three O'lary
I saw sister Mary..."

while Jane stood in the cold shadow and watched.

Mum's face poked round the back door, "Shhh." She put her finger to her lips and Bridget caught the balls, one on top of the other.

"Go and play in the street. Your dad's just getting up and he wants some peace and quiet."

They ran down the ginnel, then stood on the corner. Grey bright clouds scudded over the gasworks. Bridget did a hop-scotch up the paving-stones and back. "What shall we do now?"

But Jane only stood quietly with her hands tucked into her coat pockets.

"Come on – what shall we do now?" Bridget asked again, frowning at her. "You've got a face like a wet Monday morning."

Jane took a long time to answer. She had been thinking about it all night, but saying it was harder. "Let's go and see the egg-man."

"What!" Bridget stared at her. "Don't be daft! We only escaped by the skin of our teeth yesterday."

"No," said Jane. "I mean, let's go and *see* him. Not spying." She could not go alone. She had to find some way to make Bridget agree. "I dare you," she said quickly. "I double-dare you."

"That's not fair."

"Yes it is, so."

"But he murdered his wife! And he's mental! And he drowns cats and cuts off hens' heads and he puts poison in his eggs with a needle..." Bridget faltered before Jane's steady troubled gaze.

"That's just stupid stuff," said Jane. "If he'd really killed his wife he'd be in prison." She was less certain than she sounded.

"Not if they couldn't find evidence. Not if he'd poisoned her, or made it look like an accident!"

Jane leaned her back against the wall. A dandelion was growing between the cracks in the paving-stones. It wasn't just that she was sorry for the egg-man, she was afraid of him. But it was a different sort of fear now. What Bridget

said was just stories and she didn't really believe them – well, only a bit. Something else made her afraid of him – his talking in the empty room, his singing and chuckling, his tears, and the fresh yellow primroses on the dusty dressing-table.

Bridget gnawed at a wisp of her black hair, then she said, "If you knock and do the talking, alright." Her eyes brightened. "We might find evidence! Come on."

But Jane did not feel like smiling, or making a game of it.

Bridget said cheerily, "Anyhow, we can get some more feathers for your dad. Have you got any money?"

"A bit."

"I've got my collection – I never put it in the bag this morning. We could pretend to be buying some eggs."

It all seemed easy as they walked across the fields. Bridget would keep look out and if anything happened one of them was to run and get help. But when they stood in the lane before the blind blank house they went quiet.

"Do you really, really think he killed his wife?" Jane said.

Bridget was quiet, looking at the house. It looked as if no one lived in it, and no one ever called. It was hard to believe they had been inside. "I don't know. That's what they say..." She glanced at Jane. "I know it was a double-dare but I shan't say anything if you change your mind."

"It was him crying..." Jane said.

"I know. I was there too, remember." Then she added quickly, "Come on. We can always run."

They went up by the side of the house, openly, in view, staying close together. A sparrow was taking a dust-bath in the dry mud, watched by the kitten which was crouched on the wall.

Jane knocked stiffly on the back door. They stood side by side, and very close together. If one of them had moved they both would have run away.

"Perhaps he isn't in..." murmured Bridget.

But then they heard the soft shuffle of footsteps coming across the kitchen floor. The door creaked open and the egg-man stared at them through the narrow gap. The smells

of boiling cabbage, burned milk, and steam rushed out to meet them.

"Hello," said Jane in a very small voice.

The egg-man peered at them through his scratched and broken spectacles. His chin was prickly with white stubble and his skin was flaky on his wrinkled cheeks. "Yes?"

There was a gap of silence. Then Bridget said in a rush, "We've come to buy half a dozen eggs."

And Jane said, more slowly, and louder, "We've come to see you, Mr Black."

The door creaked a few inches wider. "Eggs, is it? Seeing, is it?" The egg-man stared through his steamed-up lenses, then, unexpectedly, he closed the door on them.

"He's still there," said Bridget. Through the dirty glass of the kitchen window she could just make out his figure, still standing behind the door. "Perhaps he's getting his axe." Bridget's eyes were like two black holes in her face, and the wind was blowing her hair across her mouth. In that instant they could have run, but the door opened again and the egg-man was standing there in his tatty jacket and worn leather slippers, carrying an egg-box in his hand. He took off his glasses, wiped them on his sleeve then hooked them back onto his ears. "Mrs Black's just popped out," he said in his quavery whisper. "I expect it's her you've come to see. You can wait in the parlour. She won't be long. I'll just get the eggs then I'll make us a nice cup of tea, eh? Yes? Tea?"

Jane looked at Bridget and Bridget looked at Jane. Perhaps Nelly Black wasn't dead after all!

"Yes, you come into the parlour, and I'll put the kettle on," whispered the egg-man.

Jane was about to step forward when Bridget suddenly caught her firmly by the elbow.

"No thanks," said Bridget. "We can't stay for tea, can we, Jane?" She gave Jane a sharp warning look. Jane was startled, but she knew Bridget was right. They shouldn't go into that quiet house, alone, with the egg-man. They might never come out again! She drew in a quick little breath.

The egg-man blinked at them then bowed his scraggy head.

Poor egg-man, thought Jane. He'd only offered them a cup of tea! She snatched her arm from Bridget's hand and frowned at her. "We'd much rather help you get the eggs, Mr Black," she said.

The old man jerked up his head again, then nodded quickly three times. "Eggs!" he crowed. "Yes, oh yes! Six fresh eggs for two bonny lasses!"

"I'm Jane," said Jane. "And this is Bridget."

"I'm very pleased to meet you," said the egg-man, and stretched out his bony fingers.

Jane bit her bottom lip. She shook hands with him and it was like shaking the cold claw of a dead sparrow.

"Free range," he said. "They're all free range. Some in the hen house and some in the long grass..."

They followed him as he shuffled through the gate and into the scruffy orchard.

The hens came scuttling and fluttering around the egg-man's feet, expecting to be fed, but he flapped his hands at them. He looked like a hen as well because his chin jerked up and down and backwards and forwards as he walked.

"Ah-ha! Tee-hee!" croaked the egg-man suddenly, reaching under a bush. He pulled out a brown speckled egg and placed it carefully in the tray. "See? These are the nicest. Oh, the very best. But you have to look carefully. Yes, yes, very carefully."

"Let's go," Bridget mouthed silently at Jane behind his back, but Jane shook her head crossly. She thought Bridget was being mean and daft.

Bridget pulled a face at her and walked off across the orchard, kicking her way through the wet grass.

Jane followed the egg-man over to the hedge. He stopped still, staring at something in the black twigs. It was Bridget's red ribbon – the one she had lost the day before.

"She's always picking flowers from the hedge," he whispered. "Losing her ribbons..." Carefully, he untangled it. It lay across his palm as bright as blood. "Bought that ribbon at Whittackers on King Street, to go with her frock... You know Whittackers? On King Street?"

Jane nodded, but she didn't know at all. It was almost as if the egg-man was talking to himself.

"Pure China silk. From the Orient, this ribbon."

Jane stared at him. He was lying about the ribbon! It was Bridget's! But he did not seem to know he was lying. He believed himself.

"It must have been expensive," Jane faltered, not knowing what to say.

"Oh yes! It was. A cruel expense."

Across the orchard, Bridget was slashing crossly at tall nettles with a stick.

"A red ribbon for a red dress," murmured the egg-man, looking at Jane. "Nothing dowdy, nothing common, not for my Nellen, eh?"

Slowly he bent and put the egg-box on the ground by his feet. He ran the silky ribbon between his fingers.

"No. No," he whispered, "nothing common for my Nell. Red's her colour..." His voice was as quiet as someone whispering in church. A bubble of silence surrounded him and Jane.

"From Whittackers, you see. Clothes for the Discerning. This Seasons's Styles from London... Only the best for my Nellen."

"Yes," whispered Jane.

The silence was like a grey cloud wrapping them both, as he held up the ribbon. The silence was like dust settling, and autumn leaves.

Clumsily and gently, the egg-man lifted Jane's plaited hair across her shoulder and began to tie the red ribbon in a bow. He laughed his whispery laugh. "A red ribbon for you, eh? Isaiah, I thought, Isaiah, that dress of Nell's needs a ribbon not a hat."

His fingers fluttered against her shoulder like a bony bird, as she remembered the red dress she had seen lying on the end of the bed, faded as a pressed-flower, with a spider's web spun like lace upon the collar.

110

Jane stood stiff and still by the black thorn hedge, as if the egg-man had pinned her with his fingertips to the ribbon, to the red butterfly of his memory.

"Oh Nellen," he whispered, and his hand, light, yet sharp as pencils, gripped Jane's shoulder. "Nellen, my Nell. You look like the fowls of heaven that maketh us wise..."

The wind gusted through the grey apple trees, rattling their branches. A dark cloud shadowed the sun, and the first spots of rain fell.

And Jane still stood silently, almost hypnotised by the old man's whispering. She was not really afraid or alarmed, because she knew it was not to her that he was speaking. For a moment she had become the ghost of Nelly Black.

"Swi-ish, swi-ish," went the sound of Bridget's stick in the nettles, but Jane hardly heard it.

"Forgive me," whispered the egg-man. Like a cold autumn leaf, his hand rested on her cheek. "I was so afraid you wouldn't come back to me..." and he bent towards her.

"Jane!" yelled Bridget. The shock of her voice cracked the silence. "Jane!" She was staring at them, white faced, from between the trees, with the stick raised in her hand.

The egg-man jerked away. Jane saw his ugly, bewildered old face like a mask, then she ran.

They slammed through the gate out of the orchard, and kept running over the fields, through the hedges, as heavy drops of rain spattered after them, until they came to the door of Jane's house. The red ribbon fell from Jane's hair and a cold gust of wind sent it fluttering over the wall like a crimson bird.

4

"THE DIRTY old beggar!" Bridget gasped. Her words punched the air. "The dirty, dirty, dirty old beggar!" She was holding Jane tightly by the arm, and they swayed in the rain on the pavement. "He was going to kiss you! He was trying to kiss you!" Bridget's words were like the wet slaps of the April wind. "The dirty, dirty . . ."

"Shut up!" Jane shouted. She shook Bridget off so fiercely that Bridget stumbled from the kerb.

Bridget stared at her until Jane felt that the mark of the egg-man's touch must be visible on her face, and even the rain could not wash it away. Her plait dripped down her shoulder. The water in the gutter gurgled over Bridget's shoes. Then she came back to Jane and stood in front of her, very quietly.

"He's just old . . ." said Jane. "He just thought I was Nellen . . . He wasn't going to . . . He didn't mean . . ." But her face felt dirty now where the egg-man's hand had touched her cheek. And Bridget would not look her in the eyes. She had seen the egg-man holding her, touching her face, bending towards her.

"Will you tell your mum and dad?"

A bicycle slissed up the wet road and came to a stop behind them.

"But he didn't do anything," said Jane.

"I think you should tell them." Bridget's face was pale and serious. Rain trickled off her chin. "He might have . . . You know . . ." Then Bridget stopped abruptly, staring over Jane's shoulder.

Her look made Jane turn, and Dad was standing by his bicycle, tugging the cycle clips from the bottom of his trousers. The shoulders of his jacket were dark with rain. "Hello, Jane," he called. "What are you doing? You'll get soaked to the skin!"

Bridget was silent.

"Coming, Dad," Jane called back, but, suddenly, she felt frightened and anxious, as if she had done something wrong and he was about to find out. "See you tomorrow, Bridget," she added quickly, in case Bridget said anything.

Bridget nodded. She turned and ran up the street towards her own house. For a moment, at the corner, she looked back. Then she was gone.

Jane glanced nervously at Dad. He had picked up his bike

ready to carry it into the hallway, and was waiting for Jane to open the door. Jane fumbled with the key. She could hardly look at him. It was as if something awful had happened, or nearly happened, or might happen. All muddled up, she felt close to tears.

"You're early," said Mum to Dad as they went into the warm room. "And you're late, miss," she added, seeing Jane.

Jane didn't say anything at all.

A look passed between Mum and Dad. Mum frowned. Dad took off his wet jacket and hung it over a chair to dry.

"Come on, Jane," said Mum, scraping the buttery knife over the bread. "Get that wet coat off before you catch your death." She watched Jane as she came to the table.

"Cheer up, poppet," said Dad, smiling at her, "it might never happen."

Jane had a sharp lump in her throat. What *had* happened? Nearly happened? Might happen? Nothing. Nothing had happened, but she felt guilty. She felt like crying.

Dad rubbed his hands on his shirt sleeves to warm himself up, and the sound was like the slither of a silken ribbon being tied in a bow.

As they sat down to tea Jane saw her Mum's hair and face with the light of the kitchen behind her, and Dad was sitting with his back to the fire, coal-gleams in his black hair, his face half in shadow and lined with tiredness. Sunday was his day off from nights, but he could never sleep properly then. He stirred his tea slowly.

"What have you been up to today then?" he asked.

"Nothing," said Jane quickly.

Mum held out the plate of bread and butter, watching Jane, then she said, "Have you and Bridget been squabbling again, love?"

"No," said Jane miserably, then suddenly realised that if she had said 'yes' it might have been better.

They were quiet for a moment.

"What is it, love?" said Mum softly. "Jane? Something's to do, I know you . . ."

Jane shook her head. She did not know why she was lying

113

– after all, it was only a daft old man who had tied a ribbon in her hair and touched her on the cheek. But she could still feel his touch. She wanted to rush upstairs and scrub her face clean. She wished she had never, never been near the egg-man's house.

Mum and Dad were both looking at her, concerned.

"It looked like young Bridget had got herself into a tizz about something..." said Dad.

"That Bridget!" said Mum, with a little laugh.

Jane put her elbows on the table and leaned her face in her hands. Her knife clattered off the plate onto the floor.

Dad shoved back his chair, crouched to pick up the knife, and then stayed on his heels beside her, with his arm round her shoulder. "Whatever is the matter, love?" he asked quietly. "Can't you tell us?"

One slow hot tear crept down Jane's face. "I don't know..." she murmured. "Bridget said he was..."

"What did Bridget say, love?"

"Bridget said he was dirty..."

Without looking at him, she felt Dad become very still beside her. His arm tightened around her. The ticking of the clock seemed to fill the room.

"Who, Jane? Who did Bridget say was dirty?" Mum asked.

Jane did not know how to tell them about the egg-man. He hadn't meant to do her any harm, she was sure, but Dad might not understand that. She pulled her face from her hands.

"The egg-man. He's mental. Everybody knows that. He thought I was his wife and tied a ribbon in my hair, because he thought it was her ribbon, but it wasn't really, it was Bridget's."

"Are you sure?" said Dad quietly. "Is that all he did?"

Jane nodded. "But Bridget thought..."

"Yes?"

"Bridget thought he was going to kiss me and she said he was a dirty old beggar."

Mum and Dad were silent.

Jane had always thought there were some things you had

to keep from adults, like their skipping song, because it embarrassed them to know that you knew what it meant. And there were some things it was easier to pretend not to understand. But now she thought she had shocked them.

"Bridget went with you, to see the egg-man?" asked Mum after a while. "You mean old Mr Black on Back Lane?" Her face in the firelight was as gentle as the picture they were making out of feathers.

Jane nodded, unhappily. "We only went to see him because we saw him crying yesterday. He didn't do anything. It was just Bridget saying... saying he was a dirty..."

"That Bridget!" said Mum. She looked at Dad, still crouched by Jane, and somehow guided him back to his chair with her eyes. He sat down but he didn't drink his tea.

"Bridget says he killed his wife. She says about the ghost of Nelly Black. I don't think he really killed her, did he?"

"No," said Mum, "he didn't kill her. What a daft idea."

"Isn't she dead then?"

"Yes. Yes she is," Mum nodded slowly. "She ran away from him, then she died in an accident. It's complicated... and it all happened a long, long time ago."

"But he didn't kill her?" Jane persisted. She had to be sure. She wouldn't feel safe again until she knew for certain that the things Bridget said about the egg-man were lies.

"No, Jane. He didn't. But he made her very unhappy, and she made him very unhappy. And then she died."

Flames licked up over the coals in the hearth and sent a warm yellow light chasing shadows up the wallpaper.

"Jane?" said Dad. "Did you go into his house with him?"

For a moment Jane did not answer. "No," she said, at last. It was the truth – they had never been in the house *with* him knowing they were there. "We went into his orchard to help look for eggs."

"Listen, lovey," said Mum, " poor Mr Black is a lonely old man. He's a funny old stick, but I don't suppose he meant you any harm, and Bridget was probably wrong. But she was right in a way, love, to be a bit frightened..."

115

"But he didn't do anything!" Jane was almost fierce now, defending herself against them misunderstanding her, and also she was defending the poor egg-man who talked to himself, and sang, and cried, in his dirty old house where no one ever went.

"No, love. He didn't," Mum sighed. "It's a rum old world, our Jane. Just because some funny old man lives alone doesn't mean he's bad or wicked. In the olden days people even thought old women and men who lived alone were witches and burned them on bonfires!"

"Your mam's right," said Dad, softly, reaching out and putting his warm hand on her wrist. "But, Jane, not everybody's good. And it only takes something bad to happen once and it could hurt you for the rest of your life. There's nowt as queer as folk, and it's the hardest thing of all to learn how to judge which are the sad ones and which are the bad ones... Aye, sad though I am to have to say it, there are some folks in this world that would harm you..." He squeezed her hand gently, then poured her a cup of tea.

"Do you know," said Mum, "when I was your age we had a teacher called Miss Peel, and she used to say, 'Girls! Pay attention girls! Never talk to strange men, and never, never, kiss one!'" Mum made her face so snooty and posh that she looked as if she was balancing a pair of steel-rimmed spectacles on the end of her nose.

Jane smiled a small smile.

"Poor old codger," said Dad. "Do you know, I'd forgotten all about him."

"Everybody's forgotten about him," said Jane, and frowned, no longer frightened, but rather sad.

That night, when she came out of the bathroom on her way to bed, Jane heard them talking quietly downstairs. Then she heard her name mentioned. She crept to the top of the stairs and sat down, with her face pressed against the banister, listening.

"Perhaps I should go and see the old fellow," she heard Dad say. "I don't know... We could tell her not to go near him in the future. He's a funny old bloke and that's a fact. If he could mistake a young lass like Jane for his dead wife – well, he might not just have. . . If anything happened to her, I'd never forgive myself."

"Oh hush you," said Mum. "It's just best left alone. I'll not have her frightened of some poor lonely old man. She's a soft hearted thing, I know – going to see him because he was crying. But she's not daft. I'll tell her to tell me before she goes visiting strangers again, but if you start scaring her with ideas like that, she'll grow up thinking all men are frightening."

"Well, I suppose you're right. Eh, dear," Dad sighed, "sometimes I think you can't win. You try and teach your child to be loving and kind, so she takes pity on a strange old bloke, then you have to teach her that sometimes a stranger can be the most dangerous thing in the world. . ."

"Fortunately, the poor egg-man isn't like that," said Mum.

"No, luckily for our Jane, Mr Black would never have meant to harm her. . ."

She heard the creak of the chair springs and the sound of someone walking across the room. Quickly she ran to her bedroom, climbed into the bed and lay very still with her eyes shut. But no one came upstairs.

For a long time Jane lay awake, staring into the dark, thinking about the egg-man. If Bridget had not been with her, what would have happened. She hadn't been scared of him when he tied the ribbon, so why was she scared afterwards?

She thought, it wasn't really me that he was talking to. It was Nelly Black. He hadn't meant to have done anything wrong. He wasn't a dirty old beggar like Bridget said. He was one of the sad ones, not one of the bad ones, but what if it had been the other way round, and she had gone there without telling anyone else first?

Poor Isaiah Black, she thought as she fell asleep, living all alone, with only a ghost and the memory of a red ribbon to keep him company.

"Jane? Jane?" someone was whispering in the darkness. "Are you awake?"

Jane pushed the sheet from her face. She saw the crack of light from her door. The hallway light was still on.

"Dad?" she whispered back.

"I thought you were asleep. . ." Dad closed the door and the room went black.

"Shut your eyes," he murmured. She did so and heard him switch on the bedside lamp. "You can open them now."

Jane blinked in the light. Dad was sitting on the edge of the bed. He smiled at her as she struggled up from the blankets. "It's very late," he said. "But I wanted to show you. Look."

He lifted the picture for her to see. It was finished. Now she was wide awake.

"Oh Dad, it's great!" And it was. It shone softly, in blues and browns and mother-of-pearl. It did look like Mum – but it looked like Mum as if she were a film star or a princess. Her face was smooth and untroubled. Her hair gleamed. There were glints of peacock red in the background as if she had been photographed by flashlight against pink velvet. And all around it was the glowing brown frame. It was beautiful – and she had helped to make it. It looked like Mum, and yet it also looked like someone who was too proud and pretty to ever hang up socks, with pegs in her mouth.

"What do you think?" said Dad. "I want it to be the best present ever."

Jane suddenly thought of the egg-man. She looked again at their picture, and now she felt a bit afraid of it. She thought of the photograph in the egg-man's living room, of Nellen Black with her cool pretty face. She stared at the picture, with the sheet twisted round her shoulder. "Dad?"

"Yes, poppet?"

"Can we give it to Mum now?"

"But it isn't her birthday until tomorrow, Jane. We don't want to spoil the surprise. And besides, she's fast asleep."

"But. . ." said Jane. She did not know how to explain the cold fear that was creeping through her. She pulled the sheet tighter, and stared helplessly at the colours of the picture until they began to blur into one soft satiny gleam. She felt cold. It was as if the ghost of Nelly Black was standing at the foot of the bed, staring down at her with eyes like frozen puddles.

She wanted Mum to have the present before something happened. She wanted Mum to have it quickly, quickly, because the egg-man had bought presents for his wife but something had happened, something terrible...

That red dress so neatly folded in the dusty room had never been worn... That red ribbon from Whittackers, had she ever got it? And those yellow primroses on her cold dressing-table – she had never seen them... Nelly Black had never come home again. And the egg-man had become a kind of ghost. He had got stuck in time, waiting for her to come back. Nellen Black was long since buried in her grave, but somehow her husband was the one who had become the ghost.

"Jane?" Dad was frowning at her. "Are you alright? What's the matter? Don't you think we've made a good job of it?" He sat on the bed beside her and let the frame rest against his knee. He was watching her, troubled.

She wanted to try and explain, but she did not know how to tell him something she hardly understood herself. It was something about real ghosts, adult ghosts. Something that made her more fearful than the ghosts she and Bridget made up. What if Mum and Dad should ever stop loving each other? What if one of them died? Or went away and never came back? And one of them was left old and whispering and alone, like the egg-man?

"Hoy? What's the matter?"

"Ghosts," said Jane in a whisper. "Bridget said the egg-man was a dirty old beggar, but he isn't. He's like a ghost."

"What?" Dad put his arm round her shoulders.

"The egg-man bought a ribbon as a present for Nellen, but I don't think she ever got it, Dad. And he still wants to give it to her – but he can't because she's dead." The words dashed out, then stopped.

"And now he's a ghost because he can't believe she won't come back, and he can't go forward any more..." And that

119

was the best way she could explain it.

"By heck," said Dad softly. "Blow me." And held her at arms length looking at her. Then, "Listen," he said.

Downstairs, the clock had begun to chime. It rang solemnly through the silent house, its hands folded on midnight. They listened as it struck twelve.

"Quick," said Dad. "Come on! Put on your dressing-gown. It's tomorrow now. It's Monday." He half lifted Jane out of bed, stood her on her feet, threw her dressing gown into her arms and then said, "Hussssh! Come on."

Jane followed him quietly, puzzled, downstairs into the darkness. The lino and carpet were cold under her bare feet.

"Get the tray from the kitchen," he whispered, turning on the table lamp. "By heck! This will give her a surprise!"

"Mum?"

"Hush," said Dad. "Yes." And he got the bottle of Christmas sherry out of the sideboard, along with three glasses.

"But she'll get mad!" said Jane. "I've got school tomorrow!"

"Today, you mean," said Dad, pointing to the clock. "She'll be furious!" and he grinned at her as he set the bottle and glasses on the tray. "Now then, I'll switch on the light, count to three, and then sing Happy Birthday at the top of your voice!"

So, together, they crept upstairs. Dad fetched the picture from Jane's bedroom and Jane carried the tray.

"Ready?" whispered Dad on the landing.

"Yes!" Jane gasped.

Dad threw open the bedroom door, switched on the light, and trumpeted, "Taarrraaa! Taranta-ranta-ra!"

Mum sat bolt upright in bed, blinking, her hair straggly with sleep and her eyes staring.

"Happy Birthday to you,
 Happy Birthday to you,
 Happy Birthday dear Mu-um!
 Happy Birthday to you!" Jane sang at the top of her voice.

"You daft...! Blooming...! Daft...! What time is it?" Mum spluttered.

"It's Monday, May the first," said Dad and kissed her smack on the nose. "Happy Birthday! Jane, pour the sherry."

Jane put the tray on the end of the bed, and carefully poured sherry into the glasses, one for each of them. She did not spill a drop. Mum was spluttering and staring and trying not to laugh, so much that Jane started laughing instead.

She gave a glass to Mum and one to Dad and took the last herself.

"A toast," said Dad.

"But it's the middle of the night!" cried Mum, struggling to free herself from the blankets without spilling her sherry. "You daft things! Jane's got school tomorrow."

"Shut up," said Dad. "I mean – Silence for the toast!" He held up his glass like an actor. And Jane did the same.

"To Mum," said Dad. "And the Queen!"

Jane said, "To Mum and the Queen!" And she and Dad drank a gulp, while Mum stared at them. "Happy Birthday."

"Oh you..." said Mum, and bit her lip.

"And now," said Dad. "Shut your eyes for your present. And put your knees down."

He put the picture on Mum's lap. "You can open them now."

"Oh, loves..." she said quietly, gazing at her picture.

"And it's got your name on," said Jane, smiling at Dad, proudly.

The look on Mum's face was better than her prettiness in the picture.

"It's lovely... And you made it..."

"Don't spill your sherry on it," said Dad.

"Is it the best?" asked Jane, climbing onto the bed. Mum nodded. "It's a first prize. It's the best ever." Then she gave them both a hug, and they all sat on the bed, looking at the present and at the feathers of her face.

There were no ghosts in this midnight room, only a happy silence, and the smell of sherry, and the three of them.

A faint breeze stirred the curtains, as if they were the hem of an old-fashioned gown. Jane thought of the egg-man, far away over the midnight fields, in the house on Back Lane, singing,

"On Richmond Hill there lives a lass
  More bright than May day morn,
  Whose charms all other maids surpass,
  A rose without a thorn..."

while in the chair beside the fire sat a woman mending a shirt with tiny delicate stitches. She was wearing a red dress and a fine new red ribbon from Whittackers on King Street which Isaiah Black had given to her that very afternoon. And, in his dreams, the egg-man smiled, kissed her on the forehead, and turned over in his sleep.

Jakey

For my Dad

THE MIST came with the tide. Across the river the seagulls swirling above the corporation tip began to fly off in ones and twos, yelping and mewing. Up river, where the town began, the tall mill chimney and the castle on the hill shivered and faded as the mist reached them. And, far off, over the November sea the sun had begun to set.

Steven sat on the stile, his hands pulled into his sleeves to keep them warm, and stared out over the ghostly marsh. He could not leave yet. He had to wait until *Rosa* appeared round the bend of the river, her engine throbbing. It was getting late. If Jakey missed the tide he would have to stay out at sea all night.

The river was silent. The marsh was grey and still, and without any sound at all save the lap-lapping of the waves as the tide crept up the muddy creeks.

Waiting for the boat made Steven lonely. He could hear the silence behind him in the trees of Freeman's Wood. He listened to the silence until he could hear it humming darkly amongst the wet black branches, and he began to be afraid.

What if *Rosa* was lost at sea? What if Jakey could not find his way back through the mist? The darkness was coming on. Soon it would be all about him, and he would be alone in this silent place of marsh and river and winter trees.

He began to have the prickly feeling that he was being watched. He glanced across the river, and his bones jumped under his skin. In the fading light a small dark figure stood, still and watchful. It had two heads.

125

Steven could not move. He stared. Then one of the heads slid down the figure's shoulder and onto the ground, and he saw it was only a boy carrying a sack, and the sack had been on his shoulder like a head. Even so, Steven could not be sure he was real. Strangers in the mist are not like other people. He waited for the stranger to move off downstream, or go back up the bank to the scrubby alder trees and long grass, but, like him, the boy seemed to be waiting.

Now there were two sounds in the still air, both so far and low that they were hardly sounds at all. One was a soft whistling and the other was the faint drumming of an engine. The drumming became louder and Steven turned from the stranger to look for the boat. He stared for it, straining, as if by looking and listening he would make the boat appear, so that the thing seemed to be happening inside him, and not out there on the curve of the river. When he glanced back the boy had vanished, like a ghost.

Now *Rosa* was coming close. Steven scrabbled out of the stile, his knees and elbows stiff with waiting, and ran to the river's edge, waving and shouting to make sure old Jakey had seen him. *Rosa's* engine went quiet. The boat glided silently to her mooring. Then Jakey came out of the wheel-house with a long pole and hooked the dripping buoy out the water. He tied a rope through a ring on the chain and let the buoy drop back into the river. Only then did the old man wave to him.

Steven waved back. He looked downstream to where the strange boy had been, or the ghost.

The old man rowed ashore in the tender, and Steven waded out to meet him. Jakey shipped an oar, grabbed him firmly by the shoulder, and hauled him out of the shallows into the little boat.

"Now then," he said.

"Hello, Jakey."

"Thick as bloomin' porridge!" said Jakey, nodding at the mist.

When they were both safe aboard *Rosa* and in her bright wheel-house, Steven began to brew the tea.

"Reckon I'll have a Two Minute Nod," said Jakey. He sat down on his chair in the corner of the wheel-house and began to snore.

Rosa smelt of oil and pipe smoke, fish blood and old sacks. It was the smell Jakey carried with him, even on land. As he waited for the kettle to boil on the primus Steven looked out over the river and into the night. He felt the soft rocking of the boat, and heard the 'slock-slock' of ripples against her wooden sides.

"What did you catch?" Steven asked when Jakey opened his eyes.

Jakey sipped his tea and pulled his pipe from his deep pocket. "Nowt." He made a noise like spitting. "I'll catch me death one of these days." He stared down at the oily planks between his big boots.

Steven saw a picture in his mind of Jakey's death swimming grey and huge in the dark deep waters of the bay, following *Rosa* like a shark. He shivered.

The old man lit his pipe and breathed a cloud of white warm smoke. "I'm an old fool, lad. There's nowt to be had back end of the year, yet I paddle out one more time, one more time. It might be me last – that's how I reckon it. But that won't bring yon flatties out of the mud with tears in their eyes!" He looked at Steven to see if he understood.

Steven nodded slowly. He tried to think of something to cheer the old man up. He remembered the stranger he had seen on the river bank. "I saw a ghost, Jakey. A ghost with two heads!"

Old Jakey looked at him for a long time. His eyes were milky blue in the wrinkles of his face. Steven could not hold his look. He shrugged.

"It gave me a right scare. But I think it was just a boy with a sack. He did look like a ghost though."

Jakey's mouth twitched. He poked the bowl of his pipe with his thumb.

"That'll be Marret, I reckon. Aye, Marret'll be back for the winter, with a sack of tailies for his ferret."

"Tailies?"

"Rats," said Jakey. "Tailies is rats, lad."

"Who's Marret?" Steven said.

"Marret is Marret, and he's a good friend of mine."

Steven stared out of the wheel-house window. He did not want Jakey to have another friend. He did not think he would like Marret.

Old Jakey gave him a narrow look. He sucked in his thin lips and pointed the stem of his pipe at Steven as if he were going to say something, but then he seemed to decide against it, and put his pipe back in his mouth.

"We'd best get on," Jakey said. "Your Aunt Lil will be fretting for thee."

"She won't," said Steven, which was the truth. They tidied up the wheel-house and made things shipshape, but they did not chat as they usually did. The idea of Jakey being friends with another boy had shut Steven up, but he thought he had said something that upset the old man. Or perhaps it was just that Jakey was tired and fed up with not catching owt and could feel his cold death swimming up river out of the deep salt bay.

"Will you be here tomorrow, Mr Jakeman?" Steven asked when they were back on the river bank and the tender was chained up on the mud. He thought he had better use the old man's polite name, just in case.

"Aye, happen. But I'll not be going out. There's more to this mist than the tide. It'll bide with us for a day or two, by the look on it."

They walked together through Freeman's Wood – sometimes old Jakey walking in front and sometimes Steven. The path was only wide enough for one at a time. Now it was black, and the mist swirled like water in the beam of Jakey's torch.

"What will you live on, Jakey, if there's no fishing? How will you get by for the winter?"

They came out of the wood behind the mill, where there was only rough waste ground between them and the street.

"Parched peas and me pension!" said Jakey, and he laughed twice like the hoot of a goose. "Get on home, lad. Tarra."

"It's not me home," said Steven quietly. "It's only me Aunty Lil's." He kicked at a stone. He did not want to go.

"Eh, I know. I know," said old Jakey gently. "But it's best not to mither her with your lateness, all the same."

"See you tomorrow, Jakey."

"Aye," said the old man. "Tarra."

"Is that you?" Aunty Lil shouted above the noise of the radio. "No, it isn't," Steven muttered under his breath. He kicked off his wellingtons without taking his hands out of his pockets. Mud splashed from his boots onto the door. He went into the kitchen with his wet socks half hanging off, leaving streaks on the floor.

Aunt Lil smiled and wiped her hands on a tea towel. "Where've you been then, love?"

"With me friend," he said. He remembered what Jakey had said about Marret, and scowled.

"Oh," she said. "Have you found yourself a nice friend then, love? That's nice." She reached down and tried to unbutton his jacket, as if he were a five year old. Embarrassed, he shook her off.

Uncle Bill looked up from behind his newspaper. "He means that daft old codger Charlie Jakeman."

Steven decided he hated Uncle Bill more than anyone else in the world, apart from Marret.

He sat down at the table. Aunt Lil put a plate of sandwiches cut into little triangles in front of him, and then a bag of crisps and a bottle of red pop. For afters there was a cake with pink icing. It all looked like party food. For the first few days after he had been sent to stay with her he had thought it was funny having party food every night for tea. Now it made him sad. Aunt Lil did not know about children. She never knew what to say to him, so she talked daft baby-talk sometimes, or she smiled a daft bright smile.

Sometimes he heard her crying when he was upstairs, and Uncle Bill would say sharp cross words. Uncle Bill sounded like a dog barking – a fierce, unfriendly dog.

"When can I go home?" he said.

"Now don't start that again, Stevie. There's a good lad. You know you can go as soon as your mam's better."

"Shane Cook says me dad's in the nick."

Aunt Lil took down the tea towel she had just hung up and held it tightly in her white hands. "Well, you tell that Shane What's-his-name to wash his mouth out! Your dad's in Germany, lad, and well you know it!"

Uncle Bill sighed. He made a great rustling fuss of folding up his newspaper and then he went out without saying goodbye to them. They heard the front door slam.

Aunt Lil's hand crept to her pale face as if she had been slapped. She saw Steven looking at her and switched on her bright empty smile again. She fussed him to eat up.

"What did you do at school today?" she asked.

"Nothing." It was the truth. It was the truth because he had not been to school, although he was meant to be there. He had hidden on the marsh instead.

"You must have done something, Steven."

"No."

"Drink up your pop," she said.

"I don't want it. It makes me feel sick." Steven heard his voice. It sounded sullen and rude. He remembered his manners. Sometimes he felt sorry for Aunt Lil. "It makes me sick, thank you, Aunty Lillian."

"Oh lovey," Aunt Lil said in a funny soft voice. "What are we to do wi' you . . ."

After tea Steven stood with his face pressed against the cold glass of the window. He had closed the curtains behind his back, so that he stood in a dark silent tent. His breath fogged the glass. He drew his name in the mist with his finger. In the street, the real mist, the salt marsh mist, made the lights and the people look as if they were under the sea. He pressed his mouth to the cold glass. He thought of Marret, and he thought of Jakey catching his death. Somehow he knew that those two things were connected, tied together in the mist with himself. But he could not understand it. He did not know why. He wondered if his mam would understand.

He drew a face in his breath on the glass. It was only a circle with two dots and a line for the mouth, but in his mind it was a picture of his mam. He looked at it, and his throat hurt in the way it hurts when you want to cry. He did not cry. Instead, he wiped out the face with a swipe of his hand.

"Look what your Uncle Bill's got you," said Aunt Lil in the room behind him. He had felt invisible behind the curtains, but she had seen his legs. He peered out of the soft private folds at her. Aunt Lil held out a comic towards him.

"Uncle Bill didn't get it. You did," he said. "I saw you." He turned back to the window and pulled the curtains tight around his shoulders. It was a lie. He had not seen her buy the comic. But it was the truth as well. Uncle Bill would never buy a comic for him. Aunt Lil had bought it and lied because she wanted him to like Uncle Bill. But he knew that Uncle Bill did not want him here.

Aunt Lil was quiet for a bit. "What did you have for dinner?" she said after a while. She was doing the ironing. The hot starchy smell of the shirts tickled his throat. .

"Parched peas!" he said. The curtains muffled his laugh.

"Parched peas?" said Aunt Lil and burnt a hole in a hanky as she stared at the humpy shape in her curtains.

"Parched peas," said Steven. "And they were lovely."

"Well I never," said Aunt Lil. "Fancy that!"

That night he dreamed about Jakey's boat. His mam was in the dream. She and Jakey were sailing over the black water and he was watching them from the shore. He saw old Jakey and his mam smiling and waving. They waved their hats. They shouted and laughed but they were too far out to sea for him to hear them. And then he saw the dark shape following the boat. A great grey shape, like a shark, swimming behind, slowly, secretly. He tried to shout to them. He tried to tell them about the great grey fish which swam behind, but his mam and Jakey were too far away to hear him above the sound of *Rosa's* engine.

Over the black sea came the salt white mist. He knew that the grey following fish would find Jakey in the mist, and his mam, and they would never hear him shouting. Then, in the dream, the strange boy came walking out of the sea, out of the mist, with a sack on his shoulder. He stood before Steven and began to open his sack to show him what was in it. But Steven sat up in bed and woke with a shout.

2

"THICK as porridge," Steven said.

"What is?"

"The mist."

Aunt Lil looked at him. "Eh," she said. "You do come out with them! Now off with you. You'll be late for school."

He ran into the white morning. It was more like swimming underwater with your eyes open than running. He looked back and could not see Aunt Lil's house across the street. He ran past the school, across the wasteground and into Freeman's Wood. He stopped among the ghostly trees. Muffled and faint and faraway came the shouts and shrieks from the playground. His breath made a cloud in the white air. In the ditch the dead grass was white as bone. He knelt to look closer and saw the frost on every winter leaf and stalk, on every twig and stone. He breathed on a twig and it blackened as the frost melted.

Slowly, he walked between the trees to the river, taking three steps forward and one step back. Three forward. One back. Until he felt dizzy with counting. He did not want to get to the boat before Jakey. Waiting was lonely.

A blackbird flew over the hedge, scolding him.

"Now then, young Steven," said Jakey. "Take a hold on this." He gave him the end of a rope.

"Hello," said Steven. "What for?"

"To make a line to hang up me nets. Used to hang them on the fence, 'til the blighters put up barbed wire." Jakey finished his knot. Then he took the rope from Steven and tied it to the stile. "There," he said. "Not at school?"

"No."

"You'll never make a scholar," Jakey said, and sat on the stile, smoking his pipe.

Steven looked across the mud. The tide was on the ebb. Something was missing. "Where's the tender?"

"Marret's gone to fetch me net and some baler-twine from *Rosa*. He's going to mend me chair."

"Marret?" Steven said. "He's gone by himself?" He peered through the mist towards the boat. Sometimes Jakey let him row the tender, but he would never have let him go out on the river by himself.

"Aye."

Steven leaned his shoulder against the tree trunk. He chewed the side of his lip. He had not reckoned on the strange boy being here. He wanted Jakey to himself. He picked up a stone and tried to skim it onto the water. But it landed with a soft 'flock' in the mud. He looked out of the corner of his eye to see whether Jakey had noticed, but the old man was staring blindly at the frozen ground.

"Thick as porridge," Steven said, to fill the silence.

"Aye," said Jakey. He lifted his head as the splash of oars and the clunk of oars in rowlocks came to them across the river. "Hoo-looo!" he hollered through his cupped hands, and winked at Steven. "He might row blind to the Irish sea."

Steven wished with all his heart that Marret would.

"Come by-yyy!" Jakey called.

The tender nosed out of the mist and up into the shallows. The boy shipped his oars and let her glide onto the mud. He jumped out and tied her to the chain, then carried the bundle of net above his head so that it would not trail in the mud. Jakey went down to help him.

Steven watched, and something in his chest tightened as if it would crack.

Marret and Jakey carried the net to the stile. As Jakey spread it the strange boy stood and looked at Steven. He had blue eyes and hair as black as melted frost on a twig. There was a streak of mud on his forehead and holes in his grey jumper. Some of the holes were darned with red wool and some with green wool. His black trousers were torn at the

133

knee and splashed with mud. He was taller than Steven. He looked at Steven and Steven could not hold his look.

"How do," said Marret. He took a ball of orange baler-twine out of his pocket then turned away. He went back to the tender and lifted Jakey's wheel-house chair out of the boat. Steven had never noticed the hole in its cane seat.

Jakey and Marret sat back to back on the stile. Jakey mending his net and Marret mending the chair. Their elbows took up a rhyme with each other's hands, knotting and twisting and threading through. Steven fretted and kicked bits of driftwood into the mud. He could not watch the birds on the river because of the mist. All he could see was what was closest to him, and what was closest to him was Marret and Jakey bent over their mending. Their work was like a curtain wrapped around them, and he was on the outside. Their work was like a secret between them and he was left out.

Steven stood in front of Jakey and said, "Why didn't you ask me to mend it?"

Jakey said, "I never knew thee could fettle a net, lad."

"No," said Steven. "The chair."

"I never knew thee could fettle a chair neither."

"Well, I wouldn't use orange string for a start."

"What would you use?" Jakey asked without looking up.

Steven thought for a moment. "Wood for a wooden chair."

"Twine's stronger and quicker," Jakey said.

Steven scowled at the boy's shoulders. Marret glanced round at him, then reached for Jakey's knife to cut the twine, and the chair was mended. Marret turned it round and sat on it, his arms folded on the back, watching Jakey's hands, He ignored Steven.

Steven picked up Jakey's knife without asking, the way Marret had done, and began to hack off slivers of wood from the stile post.

"Whoa, young Steven! Don't blunt it, lad," Jakey said, and held out his hand for the knife.

Steven wandered back down to the river and stared miserably at the grey water. When he came back Jakey and Marret were talking.

"Who are you with then?" Jakey said.

"Granny Lee," said Marret.

"Where's your old feller these days?" Jakey passed the net through his fingers looking for tears.

"Got lifted, Jakey. Starry."

"What's starry?" Steven asked, crouched in the cold grass at the old man's feet.

"Nick," said Jakey.

"Time," said Marret and he spat like Jakey sometimes did when he caught nowt.

"Prison, lad," said Jakey. "He was always a blighter for used cars."

"Nowt to do with cars," said Marret. "It was a load of non-ferrous – copper and brass and that. They said he'd lifted it – but he didn't."

"Aye, well," said Jakey. "That's his story and he's sticking to it. And he's your old feller and you're sticking to him. Lord help him." Jakey closed his eyes and pressed his fist on his chest.

Marret and Steven looked at him.

"What is it, Jakey?" Steven asked.

"Nowt," said Jakey with his eyes closed. "Take a look at me nets, Marret. I'll just have a Two Minute Nod," he whispered. He leaned his head back against the stile-post. His pipe dangled in his fingers. His face was grey in the whiteness of the mist and the frost.

Marret ran the net through his hands but his eyes never left Jakey's face.

"Are you badly?" Steven touched Jakey's cold sleeve.

Marret glared at him for waking the old man.

"It's nowt, lad."

"It's your ticker," Marret said. "I'll take you to *Rosa* and make a mash, Jakey. Nets is done."

"Eh up, lad," said Jakey. He put his hand on Steven's shoulder and pushed himself up. His weight nearly knocked Steven over. He wanted to help Jakey to the tender, but the old man shoved him gently away.

"Get off to school, young Steven. It's too cold for settin' today."

Steven stood very still, watching Marret load the chair and the net into the tender. Jakey climbed in and Marret took the oars. He pulled once, twice, three times and the mist dimmed them. Jakey waved, and then they were gone. The mist pulled a curtain of quietness over the boat and the river and Steven was left standing alone on the shore. He decided he hated no one in the world as much as he hated Marret, apart from Uncle Bill.

"I could have brewed up for him," Steven said. "And I could have mended that chair." But no one heard him.

"What's to do?" Aunt Lil said when she saw him at the door. "You're half starved with cold." She gave him a sharp look. "Have you been to school, Steven?"

"I'm fed up," Steven said.

"There, there, love," said Aunt Lil. "Don't cry. I'll make us a nice cup of tea."

"I'm not crying!" Steven said. "I'm fed up. I want to go home."

"Here, you sit by the fire. I've got some nice chocolate biscuits in the tin. We'll have a quiet afternoon, just you and me. And we'll not tell your Uncle Bill you haven't been to school. There's no point in fretting him, is there, love?"

"Would he belt me?"

"Your Uncle Bill's not in the habit of hitting small children, Steven."

"Only because he hasn't got any," Steven muttered.

"It's this mist, I expect," said Aunt Lil when she came in with the tea. "It gets everybody down. Now drink up."

"Marret's dad's in the nick."

"You shouldn't listen to rumours."

"It isn't a rumour. He told me hisself."

"Well, you keep away from him, love. Folks like that bring nothing but trouble."

"That's true," said Steven. He dipped his biscuit into the

136

steaming tea, then licked the melted chocolate. "I hate Marret," he said.

"Never mind," said Aunt Lil. "There's plenty more fish in the sea."

3

THERE WERE flowers on the window, feathery and white. In the street the mist was golden. Aunt Lil said she expected it would be gone by dinner-time, but that afternoon it was thicker than ever. She kept him at home. "Don't be so bloomin' soft!" said Uncle Bill, on his way to work, but she had her way.

"That boy's fretting," she said. "I'll not have him ill."

"Can I go and see Jakey, Aunt Lil?" Steven asked as she knelt to wash the kitchen floor.

"Well . . ." said Aunt Lil, wringing the soapy water out of the cloth.

"He's badly. It's his ticker, and I'm his only friend."

"Well," said Aunt Lil again. She wiped a shining wet sweep across the floor. "Alright then. But mind you wrap up warm."

As he put on his wellingtons she came out of the kitchen carrying a round tin. "Here, you take old Mr Jakeman that."

"What is it?"

"Damson pie. I was going to give it to your Uncle Bill for tea, but he'll not miss what he doesn't know."

Steven grinned at her. "That's two secrets we've got," he said.

"Well I never," said Aunt Lil with a little laugh. "So it is."

"Thanks, Aunty Lillian."

She stood in the doorway. He waved to her from across the street. Through the mist he saw her lift her hand.

The cold made his face burn. He carried the tin carefully. By the time he got to the river his fingers hurt with cold, and with keeping them crossed against Marret being there. It was a both-hands-crossed wish.

"How do," said Marret, stepping out from behind a tree.
Steven almost dropped the tin. He was furious that Marret
had made him jump. Marret laughed quietly. He picked his
sack up off the frozen ground and walked in front of Steven,
whistling between his teeth.

"What you got there?" Marret asked, standing astride the
stile and looking down at Steven's tin.

"Secret," said Steven. "Where's Jakey?"

"Secret," said Marret, and jumped down. He sauntered
down the river bank away from the tender which lay chained
up on the mud. That meant Jakey could not be aboard *Rosa*.

Steven stood on the stile watching him vanish into the
mist. His chest burned like ice as he watched him. The tide
was a long way down and he could see the frost flowers on
the mud, feathery and white. Strange and faint in the mist he
could hear Marret's whistling. And Marret knew where
Jakey was. "Pig. Stupid bloomin' pig!"

"Now then, young Steven. Fighting dogs come limping
home!" said Jakey behind him. "Shift off that stile and let an
old fool over."

"Jakey!"

Jakey's breath huffed in a white cloud as he climbed over.
He sat on the step and wiped his chin with his sleeve. "Eh,"
he huffed, "I'm right out of puff!"

"It's the mist, Jakey. It gets you down." Steven held out
the tin. "That's for you."

Jakey opened the tin with his thumb. "Well, bless me!
That's good on you, lad. Right good." He held the tin up to
his face and sniffed the pie. "Plum or damson?"

"Damson," said Steven.

"I've not had damson in donkey's years. I'll enjoy that."
He put the lid back on.

"Are you going out today?"

"Nay, lad. Not in this." Jakey scraped out the bowl of his
pipe with his knife and began to plug it with tobacco. Two
swans flew neck to neck low over the water. 'Whoo-whoo'
went their big wings beating on the white air. As Steven
turned to watch them he heard the scream. It was the

138

sharpest, most frightened sound he had ever heard and it brought tears to his eyes and prickles to his arms. He grabbed Jakey's sleeve. Far and near and everywhere over the marsh came the high wail.

"Don't fret theesel'," said Jakey, and patted his shoulder. He lit his pipe and shook out the match.

"What is it, Jakey?" Steven whispered.

"It's only Nipper taking a rabbit."

"Who's Nipper?"

"Marret's ferret. And yon's my supper saying confession."

Steven stared at Jakey. The silence hung like smoke across the marsh.

"That's cruel," Steven said at last.

Jakey shook his head. "It's nature. It's no different than a net of flounders or a kettle of shrimps."

"But they don't shriek!" Steven said.

"Who knows," said Jakey. "Maybe it's too soft for folks to hear."

"Ugh!" said Steven. He closed his eyes and tried to make the echo of the sound leave his head. They sat in silence, side by side. Steven could hear Jakey's breath creaking in his chest, and the whistle of his breath as he drew on the pipe.

Marret came back down the river bank. His boots crunched on the frozen grasses and the icy mud. The rabbit hung from his hand, its front paws dangling down. In his other hand he carried the sack. The bottom of the sack bulged and moved.

When he got to the stile Marret grinned at them. He held up the rabbit for Jakey to inspect. Steven looked at it for a second then he fixed his eyes on the sack instead, because he did not want to see the blood.

"By heck! He's a fair article!" Jakey said. "Aye, he's grand as owt. I'll give thee a tanner for him, Marret."

"A tanner!" Marret cried. "Don't make me laugh! Two bob, and he's cheap at the price."

Steven could tell by their voices that the bargaining was a joke between them.

139

"A shilling," Jakey said, and fetched a five penny piece out of his pocket.

"I'll clap hands on that, alright!" Marret laughed. He pulled a length of baler-twine from his pocket and tied it round the rabbit's hind legs. Then he hung it from the barbed wire. Its body was still limp and soft. Its fur was brown and flecked. The inside of its ears were grey-pink. Steven wanted to stroke its side, but he could not bring himself to look at its ripped throat. Although he hated to see the dead rabbit, he wished that he had caught it. He would have given it to Jakey, not asked for a shilling.

"Rabbit stew and damson pie! I'll live like the kings of old!" said Jakey.

Marret sat in the frozen grass at Jakey's feet. He picked a brown grass stalk and let it dangle from his mouth. There was a streak of blood on the back of his hand. The sack was between his boots, and it bulged and moved, and the ferret inside made fierce little squeaks, smelling the rabbit.

Jakey looked at the two boys. "Here," he said. "Show Nipper to Steven."

"Right-ho," said Marret cheerfully. Then he looked straight at Steven as he began to untie the string on the sack. "He bites."

Jakey chuckled. "He's not called Nipper for nowt, eh, Marret?"

A pointy yellow head poked out of the sack. It blinked pink eyes and made a snuffling squeak. Pink paws scrabbled at the sack. Its fur was yellow as honey, and its nose was pink as soap. It blinked at Steven, then tried to wriggle the rest of its body out of the sack. Marret grasped it firmly by the scruff of the neck. The ferret snuffled, wriggled, and yawned. There was a dab of red round its jaw. It had sharp white teeth, white as bone, sharp as pins. Marret said something to Nipper, softly, but he never let go. Nipper licked his tiny sharp teeth.

Without thinking, Steven stretched out his hand. Nipper's fur looked soft.

Jakey's big hand shot out and caught him by the wrist. "Eh

up! He'll have thee!" He let Steven go. Steven put his hand in his pocket.

"Them's all belly and teeth," Jakey explained. "And his belly's empty."

"No it ain't," said Marret. He stuffed Nipper's snakey head back in the sack and pulled the string tight. "If you hunger them before they go down a hole they'd stay and eat what they catched. You'd never get the blighter out. He'd stay in the hole and stuff hisself, then curl up asleep."

Jakey nodded thoughtfully. He put another match to his pipe. "Aye. There's an art to it alright." He looked at Steven. "This feller knows all there is to know about ferrets, I reckon. And what he doesn't know isn't worth breath asking."

Jakey knew fish and Marret knew ferrets. Steven looked at the ground, knowing nothing.

"Aye," said Jakey. "Ferrets and lurcher dogs."

Marret shook his head. "It's my old feller's the one for the dogs. Not me. Him, and old Batey Smith."

Two herring-gulls glided out of the mist, flapped their wings once, twice, and vanished again into the salt air. The old man gazed after them for a very long time, his thoughts gone with them to the shoals and sandbanks and the deep water channels of the bay.

"Bet I can lob a stone further than you," Steven said, looking at Marret.

"How much?"

Steven felt in his pocket and found tuppence. "That much," he said.

Marret smiled slowly. "Tuppence to my shilling. You're on. Best of three chucks." He got slowly to his feet and spat into his hands.

Steven's heart sank. He looked at Marret and knew he was going to lose. He trailed after him to the water's edge and picked up three pebbles. Marret spent a long time choosing his stones.

"You first," Steven said.

Marret's arm went through the air with a crack. The stone flew straight and out and halfway across the river. It splashed, and the ripples carried away the rings. Steven chucked his pebble. It went high high up, and came down behind Marret's. Marret grinned, and began to whistle softly between his teeth. Crack, splash, the second stone went further than his first.

Furious, Steven let go with his, gasping with the throw. His pebble passed the place where Marret's first had splashed, and landed in the ripples that ringed Marret's second throw.

"Nearly," said Marret. "But not quite. I win."

"Not yet, you don't. Best of three. Lob your last 'un!"

Marret laughed. He took three steps back then ran them forward. Crack, whizz, the stone shot through the mist, skimming the water and landed without a sound in the soft mud of the far river bank. "I win," said Marret. He shoved his hands into his pockets and turned away, not waiting to watch.

Steven swung his arm with all his strength. The stone flew from his hand. He willed it across the river, his teeth biting into his lip. Splash. In the water. Close to the far shore. But not close enough. Marret had not watched, and Jakey was staring off down river. His heart beat a double, stopped, and doubled again. He clenched his fist. "No you don't," he said. "I beat you."

"Give over," said Marret, looking back. "That's tuppence you owe us. Hand it over."

"I won," said Steven, his face burning with the lie. "My stone went into the grass. You owe me a shilling. I won. I won!" He had said it now. It was too late. He could not back down. What if Jakey had seen after all? It was too late. Too late.

Marret came back to the water's edge and took his hands out of his pockets. "Liar," he said quietly into Steven's hot face. The word was a white cloud between them. "Liar."

Steven's hands shot up, ready to fend Marret off. But Marret only looked at him, his blue eyes deep and still and black a long way in.

"You can keep your flamin' tuppence! I don't need your stinking cash." Then he walked back to Jakey, leaving Steven alone in the frozen mud.

Steven saw the boy's back, the stiff way of his shoulders with the anger in them. He watched Marret swing up his sack and nod to Jakey. The old man reached out a hand as if to stop him, and Marret shrugged, shook his head, spat into the long grass of the ditch. He did not turn round. He did not look back. He swung himself over the stile and strode away through the ghostly trees, until the mist hid him. And the silence he went in was the worse thing Steven had ever known. Jakey hunched on the stile in the frozen air, his hand to his face. And Steven could not go to him to explain what had happened. He had lied, he had lost. He could not lie to the old man, and lose everything, for ever and always. It was worse than being shouted at by his mam, worse than his dad not being there for his birthday. The hurt of what he had done was colder than stone, deeper than the salt water of the bay, clinging as mist.

Before Jakey could look at him, he ran. Ran, ran slipping and stumbling away from the river – sharp frozen grass whipped his hands, crunched under his boots. Running and scrambling upstream and a way he did not know. Over the broken wall, over the frozen puddles of the waste ground by the mill. In a lost country between the marsh and the street. Lost, he looked for a path. But all he could see in the mist was what was closest, and what was closest was always the same. Broken bricks on the ground, frozen puddles, smashed and jagged as broken windows, the white air twenty steps away, his own cloudy breath.

And in his mind he saw Marret walking away, gone for-ever, the sack on his shoulder. And Jakey, hunched and grey, waiting to catch his death. Nothing else. No one else.

And then he was out, suddenly, through an alley onto the street opposite the school. Muffled and faint, though really so near, came the shouts and shrieks and laughs from the playground. All the other kids yelling on the inside, and him on the outside, gulping for breath.

A football came flying over the tall wire fence onto the road. Thud tap-tap-tap. It rolled into the kerb. Steven ran on before anyone came after it. Up the street his boots clattered, and across the road. The numbers of the houses came at him out of the mist, until he came, at last, to Aunt Lil's. Then he dropped down onto the doorstep, and he stayed there for a long time, still as stone, and cold.

"Eat your tea, Steven," said Aunt Lil, for the sixth time since he had sat down at the table.

"Leave the lad alone," said Uncle Bill. He stirred three spoonfuls of sugar into his mug. "He's got enough on his plate as it is."

4

NEXT DAY, the mist had gone, and so had Jakey. The sky was one grey cloud, and a bitter wind blew litter along the black pavements. The mist and the frost, Jakey and Marret, they had all vanished, and there was no sign that they had ever been. Only a few tufts of rabbit fur, soft and brown, were caught in the barbed wire. *Rosa* swung on her mooring in the lonely river and the tender lay on its side in the mud.

The seagulls circled over the tip and the marsh grass rippled like brown water in the wind.

There was nothing to do but wait, until at last Steven knew that waiting was useless. No one would come. He did not know where Jakey lived, and even if Marret was here, he was sure Marret would not tell him.

He almost wished he had gone to school. He could not go now because he would be told off for being late.

The wind rattled the hawthorn twigs and was colder than the frost. Then drizzle drifted up with the tide. Chilly and damp, Steven turned back. He walked slowly between the trees, up the thin path through Freeman's Wood. There was no one to walk in front of him, and no one to walk behind. He pulled his hands into his sleeves to keep them warm, but it did not help much. The wind blew through his jacket and made his back feel thin with cold.

He did not want to go to school, and he did not dare go

back to Aunt Lil's. The only place he could think of where he wanted to be was his mam's. And that seemed so long ago, and so far away, that it was hard to remember how it had been. Further and farther still was last Christmas, when his dad was at home. He tried to reckon the times inbetween. July, he had come to Aunt Lil's, and it was nearly December now. Six months since he had seen his mum. Nearly a year since he had seen his dad. It could have been a hundred years. Even a million. Home was an impossible time away. Like trying to imagine the space between stars.

He tried whistling between his teeth, the way Marret did. But all he got was a hiss, and not the soft low music of the strange boy's breath. He tried again. Then he heard it. Somewhere close, through the trees. When he listened the whistling stopped, so he thought he had imagined it. Then it started again. Stopped. Started. And all the while Steven stood still, his heart beating loud over the music.

As quietly as he could, he made his way up the black bank between the roots of the trees. The dark smell of earth and leaves filled his nose and mouth. Then he saw Marret, bending, whistling, quiet, to pick up a stick, or to poke the earth with the long branch he held in his hand.

Steven stayed quiet, hidden. Watching.

"How do," said Marret, without looking up.

Steven grinned and scrambled up the bank. "How do."

Still without looking at him, Marret said, "You owe me tuppence."

Steven reached in his pocket. "Here," he said. He held it out. "Please."

Marret took it. He went on poking with his branch, picking up sticks and putting them in a pile.

"Don't you go to school?" Steven asked at last.

"I'm no scholar," said Marret. "Here, cop hold of these." He pointed to his bundle of sticks.

Steven did as he asked. "Where do you want them?"

"By that big pile under the thorny tree."

"I'm no scholar neither," said Steven when he came back.

145

"Yes you are. Jakey said so," Marret made a scratch in the black earth with his branch. "What's that?"

Steven looked at it. "That's M – for Marret."

The boy smiled. "Muh for Marret. Jakey showed me that." Then Marret stuck his tongue between his teeth and concentrated hard. He drew another shape. "What's that?"

"U – for umbrella."

"No it ain't!" cried Marret. "It's a one legged horse!" Then he laughed and laughed, leaning his shoulder against a tree.

Steven laughed a bit as well. Then he said, "Me dad's in the nick like your old feller."

Marret stopped laughing. He crouched down, resting his hands round the branch and looked for a long time at Steven, out of the black depths of his eyes.

"Where is he?" he said at last.

"Dunno. Germany, I think."

Marret thought about this. "Is that near Durham?"

Steven shrugged. "It's over the sea. A long way. Further than Manchester. Further than the Isle of Wight even!"

Marret banged his branch into the earth a few times, thinking. Then he nodded. Now that he was with Marret the wind seemed less cold, and amongst the trees there was less rain.

Steven crouched down too, watching Marret. Marret was like a grown-up, knowing things, with his face still and watchful.

"If you give us a hand, I'll give you a penny back," Marret said. He took the ball of baler-twine out of his pocket and held it out to Steven.

"What shall I do?"

"Tie them kindlings, them twigs, into bundles like them over there."

"Alright."

"That's if you can tie a fast knot."

"Easy," said Steven. "Jakey showed me how."

Marret held out his other hand. In it was a small shiny knife. "You cut the lengths. Then give it us back."

So Steven spent the morning cutting and binding and

knotting. And Marret collected the sticks, all of them smooth and round and the same, and broken to length with his foot.

Marret came over and knelt beside him, watching him tie the last knot.

"What are they for?" Steven asked, looking at the bundles.

"Kindling. Firewood. For me Granny Lee to flog." He picked up the knife and wiped the blade on his sleeve. "That's me lot. That's all I can shift."

"Does your Granny Lee have a shop?"

Marret laughed. "No! She hawks sticks to flatties."

"What are flatties?"

"You're a flattie."

"I'm not a flattie!" Steven said angrily.

But Marret just looked at him, his head on one side, and his eyes dark and still all the way in. "Here's the penny I owe you."

"Ta. Alright, if I'm a flattie, what are you?"

Marret did not answer straight away. His voice was quiet. "I'm a traveller. And this here wood, this place where we are, is where I was birthed. Me mam came collecting sticks, then tide comes up and she can't get back over. So she had me here. And four days later that birthing killed her stone dead."

Steven listened. Marret was not like a boy at all. He was like Jakey. His voice was like Jakey's voice – not old, but full of quiet, strange things. Things come from an old time or far away. And he carried a quietness in him where the darkness behind his eyes led.

"I was born in Preston Royal Firmary – but I don't rightly remember it," Steven said. His mam was in hospital there now, still poorly with her bad back. Thinking of that made him remember Jakey again. "Where's Jakey?"

"Took to his bed," Marret said. He began to tie all the separate bundles of wood into one big bundle which he could carry.

"Where does he live?"

"Secret."

"Go on," said Steven. "Tell us. And I'll give you a penny."

"Done!" said Marret. "First, give us a bunk up with this."

147

Steven helped him heave the stack of wood onto his shoulders. Marret shrugged it up until it was even and comfortable on his back. On the ground the sticks had seemed too many to be lifted, but on Marret's shoulders they seemed less, because he had the trick of tying and carrying.

"Go on. Tell us then."

"Give us the penny first, flattie."

Steven handed it over.

"He lives in a house," Marret said and walked off with his bundles.

"Hey! That's cheating! Tell me! You said you'd tell me!" Steven ran after him, cheated, shouting. "Tell me! Or give us me penny back!"

"You asked, and I told you," Marrett said. He kept walking. "Now we're even-stevens." He was on the path now, and the sticks filled it. Steven hopped behind him, shouting. He wanted to hit him, but he could see how heavy the bundle was and he was afraid of toppling Marret into the ditch. Besides, he was scared of what might come out of his dark, dreaming eyes. And it was fair. He had tried to cheat Marret yesterday with a lie. Now Marret had cheated him with half the truth.

He stopped shouting and followed behind, quietly. They came out into the rain on the river bank.

Marret put the bundle of sticks into the tender and began to untie her.

"Hey! You can't take Jakey's boat without asking!" Steven cried, grabbing at the rope.

"What makes you think I haven't asked? Me and Jakey have got an arrangement. Now leave go, or I'll belt you."

Steven let go. He watched Marret shove the tender into the shallows and fit the long oars. "If I come tomorrow, will you tell us where Jakey lives?"

The boy nodded. "You never know, he might be here hisself."

"But if he isn't, you'll tell us?"

"Might do," said Marret. And he rowed away to the far river bank, his load of kindling spiky and tall in the belly of the tender.

Uncle Bill was waiting for him when he got in. "Where've you been?"

"School," said Steven. His face felt hot.

"Pull the other one, it's got bells on!" said Uncle Bill. His newspaper was folded tight in his hand and he kept tapping it against his knee.

"Bill," said Aunty Lillian. "Please..."

"No!" barked Uncle Bill. "You let him stay at home yesterday and all this young blighter does is take advantage of your soft heart! School! He's not been near the place for days! Have you, lad?"

Steven stared at the pattern on the carpet.

"Well, answer me, lad!" Uncle Bill said. "What have you got to say for yourself?"

"It's not me real school," Steven murmured. "And it's not me home here."

"Oh! Ho-ho!" Uncle Bill cried. "I see. We're not good enough for you then, lad! Your Aunty Lil's been working her fingers to the bone looking after you and this is your idea of gratitude, is it?"

Steven stayed where he was by the door, staring at the red and purple flowers in the carpet.

Aunty Lil was standing by the table with a plate of sandwiches in her hands. The kettle was boiling in the kitchen, filling the room with steamy mist.

"Well? I'm waiting, lad," Uncle Bill said. "I haven't got all night."

"I went to see Jakey," Steven whispered. "But he never come. He's took to his bed."

"Oh, did you now?" said Uncle Bill. "And I suppose it wasn't you that Fred saw talking with that tinker lad?"

"Tinker?" said Aunt Lil.

"You keep out of it, Lillian," Uncle Bill snapped.

"What tinker?" said Steven.

"What tinker? Hark at him! What bloomin' tinker! You know very well who I mean. Fred saw you with that gypsy lad by the river, plotting some mischief no doubt. I'll not have it, do you hear! There's enough bad blood in this family without it rearing its ugly head in my house! Well, I'll tell you, lad, it doesn't come from your Aunt Lil's side of the family!"

"What doesn't?" said Steven.

"Bill! That's enough!" said Aunt Lil. Her voice was sharp and surprising. Even Uncle Bill looked at her.

"Alright, alright," said Uncle Bill. "But you listen to me, lad. If you're not at school tomorrow, there'll be real trouble. Real trouble! Do you understand?"

"Yes, Uncle Bill," Steven muttered.

"Well, Bill," said Aunt Lil. "That's all very well. But if he goes to school tomorrow he'll be the only one there. Tomorrow's Saturday."

Uncle Bill opened and shut his mouth with a snap. And, for the first time, Steven really knew that Aunty Lil was on his side.

"Now," said Aunty Lil. "You get your tea, Steven. But you listen to your Uncle Bill. You've got to go to school. It's the law. And as for tinkers – our Lord Jesus was born in a stable and spent most of his life on the road."

Uncle Bill stared at her. Then he unfolded his newspaper and held it up in front of his face.

"Marret was born in Freeman's Wood," said Steven, following her into the kitchen. "And it killed his mam stone dead."

"Oh lovey," said Aunty Lil. "That's as maybe. But you still should have been at school."

"Sorry," said Steven, because he could see she was upset.

"Did you hear that, Bill? Steven said 'sorry,' " she called through to Uncle Bill.

"And well he might!" growled Uncle Bill from behind his newspaper.

5

"THAT'S where Jakey lives." Marret pointed across the rubble and broken bricks.

"Don't be daft," said Steven. "That's an old mill, not a house."

"It is what it is!" said Marret angrily. "And Jakey lives there by the gate." He walked on quickly passed the silent bulldozers. Half the old mill lay shoved in a heap by their metal teeth, and half still stood, battered and jagged. Two dogs sniffed around the ruins.

Marret was right. There was a tiny house by the gate. The house was built into the high mill wall, though now the wall was cracked and cob-ended. A bulldozer was parked by it, its bucket full of bricks and mortar.

"Heck!" said Steven. "What if they bulldoze his house?"

"That's what they want to do," Marret said. "But he won't shift."

They came to the door. There was cardboard stuck over the window and some planks were nailed over a hole in the door. It did not look as if anyone could live there at all. It was not what Steven had imagined. He knew Jakey lived by the river and had pictured a cottage right on the river bank, with a garden and a wooden gate, and a seagull sitting on the chimney.

Marret banged with his fist. "Hey! Jakey! It's us!" He pushed open the door and went into the dark.

"Now then," said Jakey. "If it isn't young Steven and Marret! Come in, lads, and put wood in' hole."

Jakey was sitting in a chair by the fireplace, with a rug wrapped round his legs and one wrapped round his shoulders. The hearth was cold and black and full of grey ashes. As his eyes became used to the dark, Steven saw that the room was full of sacks and kits and old fish crates. There was a broken oar propped in the corner and a hurricane-lamp hanging from a hook in the ceiling. On the mantel-shelf stood a rack of pipes, a stack of tobacco tins and four big glass floats like giant green marbles.

The room smelt of old sacks, fish blood, and pipe smoke. It was the smell of *Rosa's* wheel-house, and of Jakey.

"Pull up a pew," Jakey said. But there wasn't another chair in the room. Marret dragged a crate over to the hearth, and Steven turned a bucket upside down and sat on that.

"Your fire's gone out," said Marret.

"Aye. Out all night and all day, and I'm an old fool without gumption to get it lit again."

"I'll light it," said Steven.

"Good lad," said the old man. "There's wood out the back, if these blighters from the Council haven't chucked it all on their bonfires. They've been at it three weeks now – bulldozing and burning, roaring and smoking. But they've not shifted this dog from the manger. Eh, Marret?"

"Come on," said Marret. "We'll get some wood easy enough. There's tons out there. Lend us your axe, Jakey."

"It's by the door."

Marret picked up a sack, and Steven took the axe. They went out onto the heaps of bricks and mud where jagged planks were cracked in splinters as long as their arms. It did not take long to fill the sack. Steven smashed the broken ends of planks with the axe, and Marret stamped the splinters to kindling with his boots. Marret's face was dark and frowning as he worked. But Steven swung the weight of the axe high and crashed it down, grinning. It was the first time he had used a real axe. Its weight was wonderful in his two hands. "Here comes the chopper to chop off your head!" he shouted, chopping the ground with each word.

"Give over!" cried Marret angrily as bits of brick and stone shot everywhere.

"Or what?" said Steven, standing his ground, with the axe in his hand, full of its weight and its power.

But Marret ignored him. "Come on. Let's get this fire set before Jakey freezes to death."

"Anyway," said Steven, "who rattled your bloomin' cage?"

"He never," said Marret. Stamp. "Let his," Stamp. Crack. "Fire go out." Stamp. "Last winter." Crack. He picked up the broken bits of wood and looked at Steven. And Steven realised that Marret was not being bossy, but sharp, the way his mam was when she was upset.

They took the sack back to Jakey's house. Steven lit the fire and Marret brewed a pot of tea.

"Grand," said the old man, warming his grey hands round the mug. The flames filled his face with deep shadows. Steven sat back on his heels and looked at him. The shadows made black lines round Jakey's mouth and across his forehead. He looked thinner and smaller than he had done two days before. Now it was Steven's face that was dark and frowning as he looked at his friend, and saw the oldness whittling him away.

"Eh up, Steven?" said Jakey. "What's to do?"

"Nowt," said Steven. He dropped another piece of wood into the flames. Already the sack was half empty. "I'll go and chop some more wood, Jakey. To last you."

"Well don't go daft," said Jakey. "I reckon I'll be seeing enough of fires in the hereafter."

Marret jumped to his feet. "Don't talk daft!" he cried. He grabbed the axe and rushed outside.

Steven was about to follow him, but the old man shook his head. "Leave him be. You tell us how things are on the river, eh? And pass us me pipe off the shelf."

As they talked they could hear the thud of the axe, and its sound was lonely and sorrowful in the still, cold day.

"What's it like, being old?" asked Steven, staring into the red flames.

"Wait and see, lad," Jakey said. "Wait and see..."

Steven could not imagine it. He had never thought of himself, one day, being old as Jakey. "The mist has gone," he said. "I thought you might have gone out in *Rosa*."

"To catch me death?" Jakey chuckled. Then he was quiet. "I might, young Steven. I might."

Darkness was coming on, but now Jakey's room was warm and bright with the fire. Marret came in with two full sacks of wood, big lumps which would last longer than sticks and splinters. They had another mug of tea and finished the

153

rest of the damson pie. Then Steven and Marret washed up and emptied the teapot. Jakey closed his eyes and leaned his head back against the chair.

"See you tomorrow, Jakey," Steven said.

"Happen," said the old man. He opened his eyes and smiled at them. "Bless you both. Tarra."

They went quietly over the rough ground, where the dark shapes of bulldozers crouched amongst the ruins. Steven was glad Marret walked beside him and though they did not speak to each other, they shared the silence.

"I'll meet you down at the stile tomorrow morning," Steven said, when they came to the path.

Marret nodded. He pulled at a loose thread in his tatty sleeve, as if he did not want to go. "I've never seen Jakey so badly," he said softly. "See you tomorrow, flattie, but if you're not early I'll go on without you."

"That's alright. I can find me own way now. But I'll be here. Tarra."

Steven ran off down the path, leaving Marret among the cold trees.

Aunt Lil had got a letter from his mam. "Listen to this," she said. "This should cheer you up, Steven." She held the letter up and read, "'The doctor says I am on the mend and I can go home on Tuesday. Tell Steven he can come home on Friday next'! – There! What do you think of that?"

Steven did not say anything. He thought of his mam, then he thought of Jakey and Marret. All the autumn, all he had wanted was to go home, but now he was not so sure.

"Well?" said Aunt Lil. "Isn't that good?"

"Yes, but..."

"But what?"

"Nothing," said Steven.

"Eh, I don't know," said Aunty Lil, folding up his mam's letter. "You're a queer kettle of fish, and that's a fact. I thought you'd be pleased."

"I am pleased," Steven said.

"Well you've got a funny way of showing it," Aunty Lil said.

Uncle Bill looked up from behind his newspaper. "Leave the lad alone. One minute you're fretting because he's not settling in and the next you're fretting because he doesn't want to go. If you ask me, you're a right pair of kippers!" For the first time since he had come to stay with them, Uncle Bill looked at Steven and smiled.

Steven guessed that Uncle Bill would be glad to see the back of him. He scowled back. But Uncle Bill did not seem to notice.

"Choose us a winner for the three-thirty," he said. "Starry Bright, Alan's Lad, or Rosa Gallica." They were names of horses running in the race.

"Rosa," said Steven.

"Rosa it is! And at twenty to one she's an out and out outsider."

"She'll win," said Steven.

"Really, Bill," said Aunty Lil. "Don't encourage the boy to gamble."

Uncle Bill took a stub of pencil from his pocket, licked the tip, and winked at Steven.

Steven was so surprised that he winked back, and Uncle Bill laughed quietly as he underlined the name.

As he lay in bed in the dark Steven thought about Jakey and his mam. He wanted to go home, but he did not want to leave his old friend in his small cold room with the bulldozers roaring and crunching up the walls around him. He thought of *Rosa*, forlorn on the winter tide, and Marret with his sack on his shoulder and his dark, lonely eyes. Marret had seen something that he had not seen until then. Jakey's death was swimming up river out of the deep dark waters of the bay. Jakey knew and Marret knew. And now he knew it, as he lay there alone. It was like the mist – it came so quietly, so stealthily. It was like the tide coming in, once and forever.

Marret had Nipper and his Granny Lee, and he had Uncle Bill and his mam, but Jakey had only himself. "And us," Steven said aloud.

He climbed out of bed and went to the window. Between the chimney pots and roof tops were sparkling cold stars, frost white. Frost and mist, year in, year out, tides and turnings, quietly passing. This was Jakey's death coming and Steven had no fear of it now. He went back to bed and pulled the sheet up over his shoulder. And he slept without dreaming.

6

A HERON glided down onto the mud, folded its wings and stalked into the shallows. Steven stood by the stile, watching. It was early morning. And *Rosa* had gone. The river was wide and empty. The tide was almost out. The tender rocked in the far shallows, adrift.

"Bloomin' heck!" Steven said, thinking Jakey had gone out to sea and taken Marret with him for the ride. But, even before he saw Marret come up through the tall grass and scramble down the far river bank, he knew that was not so. Jakey had gone to catch his death, and he had left the tender for them.

Marret waved. He waded into the river to catch the tender's trailing rope. He pulled it close then rowed across. The heron lifted and flapped away, low over the salt marsh on grey slow wings.

Marret was smiling. "Jakey must have gone out," he said, as he stepped ashore.

"Yes," said Steven, "He's gone." He watched the heron glide and turn across the winter sun. Everything was still. He looked at the mud between his boots and saw a footprint filling with water. A big footprint, and another one further down, the measure of Jakey's stride. Twice as big as his own, gone to the tide.

"Give us a hand," Marret said. Steven tied the tender's rope to the chain as Marret lifted his sack ashore.

Then Steven went and sat on the stile. Shreds of grey ash from Jakey's pipe lay scattered in the grass beneath the step. That was all there was – footprints sinking softly away. Cold ash. The white morning.

Jakey

Marret came up to him, carrying his sack.

"If he went on the night tide he'll be back before dinner."

"No," Steven's voice hurt in his throat. "I don't reckon he'll be back."

"Don't talk daft!" Marret said. He let the sack slide gently from his shoulder with the bulge and curve of Nipper in its folds. "Shove over."

Steven made room for him on the step.

"I've got some bread and some baccy. That's what I got belted for." Marret lifted his face to show Steven the bruise on his cheek.

Steven saw the bruise. He wanted Marret to go away. *Rosa* had gone. The tide would turn and turn again and wash Jakey's footprints away. But neither *Rosa* nor Jakey would come back.

Between Marret's boots the sack squirmed and shuffled. Marret bent to it. He murmured something in a soft voice as he untied the string. Then Nipper was flowing up into his arms and over his lap like water, like a ripple of yellow foam.

"Hushtie, hushtie," Marret murmured, running his brown fingers into her yellow fur, finding the scruff of her snakey neck. The ferret scrabbled at his torn sleeve. Marret bent his bruised face over her, but he held her firmly. He began to whistle a far away tune between his teeth, soft and low, with only the distant curlew to call back, and the piping redshanks on the shoals.

"Marret," said Steven. "I think Jakey's gone."

"What do you know!" Marret cried angrily. "What do you know about anything, flattie?" He shoved Nipper roughly back into the sack and walked quickly to the tender as if he were going to row away.

But Steven waited for him to come back, because he knew he would. There was nowhere to go. Jakey's death was in all the white morning, still and peaceful as the marsh grass, quiet as the river.

It was quiet as sleeping, patient as winter. Jakey had gone out one last time, and the only hurt was in Marret who had been left behind. The hurt was like Marret's tatty jumper,

157

Jakey

full of holes that wanted mending. And Steven knew then
that Nipper was not like having an Aunt Lil or an Uncle Bill
or a mam to go back to. Marret was like Jakey. He had no
one else. Jakey was all he had, and Jakey had gone. Marret
did not want to believe it.

At last Marret came back to the stile. He was not
whistling. He did not look up.

"We'll wait and see," Steven said quietly.

"No." Marret shook his head. When he looked up his face
was thin and his eyes dark as water you could drown in.

"Look," said Steven. "Jakey wanted to go. He didn't come
down here for nowt."

"Yes," said Marret.

It was like telling a story. A special story – every word had
to be right. "He come down last night – special, to catch the
tide. He smoked his pipe, see." Steven pointed to the ash on
the ground. "And then he sat a bit. You mended his chair and
his nets – so he knew they was right."

Marret nodded. His eyes were hungry, were full of holes
that wanted mending.

"Then tide come up." Steven shut his eyes to imagine.
"Right black. With stars. And Jakey was all breathing white
and blowing his pipe."

"Yes," said Marret. He sat on the step by Steven and held
his sack on his knee. "Bet he was scared of the dark."

"Heck!" said Steven. "Only a bit. But he had his torch
what he could switch on when he was right scared."

"Yes."

"Jakey switched on his torch. And he put his pipe in his
pocket." Steven's voice hurt. He saw Jakey. Jakey in the dark
under the frosty stars. *Rosa* black on the river. Black ripples
on the mud. The long thin light of the torch shining and
shining and wobbling in his hand.

"Then he got in the tender."

"And he put oars in them things," said Marret, pointing.

"And he got on *Rosa* and he gave tender a right good shove
so it'd stay."

"And he sat on his chair."

158

"And he turned on the engine. In the dark. And that was that..."

"No," Marret said. "Jakey oiled his winch, and put nets on, and he stacked all them boxes and he brewed up, and he walked his inspection, and he took the buoy out of the water with his stick and he untied the rope, and then he sat on his chair and put his hands on the wheel, and he went out... thinking on his house and his fire what we lit..." Marret was silent for a good bit then. "His fire what we lit."

"And Jakey..." Steven said.

"And Jakey," Marret said. "And Jakey," Marret cried, "wouldn't come back if you bloomin' paid him!"

And then they were so silent that the heron returned. They were so still they could hear the river rippling past as the tide crept back. Nipper slept in the sack, warm on Marret's knee.

"I'll stay," said Steven. "If you'll stay." It was getting dark.

"I'll stay," said Marret. "But I'll get belted."

"So will I."

"Let's go to Jakey's house."

"Alright."

Steven's hands ached with cold, and the white winter morning had become a silent, misty afternoon. Now the tide had swollen the river again.

They hurried past the rubble and the ruins and the big crouching bulldozers to Jakey's house. Marret pushed open the door. Inside, the smell of Jakey was there like a ghost – pipe-smoke and old sacks and fish blood.

Marret went and stood by Jakey's empty chair. "Reckon they'll bulldoze Jakey's house now."

"Yes," said Steven. Jakey had gone and *Rosa* had gone and now the little cold house would go as well.

"We've got to shift next week. Council gaffer says we're to move on." Marret stroked his hand along the back of Jakey's chair. "I didn't tell Jakey." He glanced around the room.

"I'm going, Friday next," said Steven. "I didn't tell Jakey neither."

"Cop hold of this," Marret passed Steven Jakey's pipes off the mantel shelf. "And this." He handed Steven Jakey's mug.

"You can't take them!" Steven said.

"I'm not lifting them, but I'm not leaving them for the Council gaffers neither. We'll take 'em to the river. For Jakey."

"But..." said Steven. But Marret was already unhooking Jakey's hurricane lamp from the ceiling, and filling his pockets with Jakey's old tobacco tins.

"But..." said Steven. But Marret just handed him the big axe from by the door.

"Get a move on, flattie. Come on! Shift!" Marret said, grabbing the sack with Nipper in it. Then he ran, his pockets and his jumper bulging with the mug and the tins and the green glass floats, and the hurricane lamp swinging from his hand.

Steven ran after him, carrying the heavy axe, afraid of falling on it. They ran through the misty twilight, over the sharp bricks and sudden mounds, and through Freeman's Wood, until they came to the stile, bursting for breath.

Marret left Nipper on the stile. He went down to the mud and pulled the tender ashore. Steven followed him. The tide had covered Jakey's footprints, washed them away.

Marret put the tins and the mug, the lamp and the floats on the tender's wooden seat. He took the axe from Steven and propped it in the bow. It was almost dark now, grey-dark, and sea gulls wheeled overhead and then flew off in ones and twos, yelping and mewing. The alder trees on the far river bank were ghostly in the mist.

Marret took the parcel of bread wrapped in newspaper from his sleeve, and the twist of tobacco. He put them in the tender as well.

"Here," said Steven. He felt in his pocket for the penny, and Marret put it on the seat beside the lamp.

Steven stood quietly, watching, as Marret untied the rope. Marret was grey and still as a heron, and then, suddenly, he tossed the rope into the belly of the tender and gave her a great shove out into the river, splashing in after to shove her further. He stood up to his knees in the chilly river as the tide, turning, turned her. The tender drifted side on to the current.

Steven willed her to turn, to face the sea and follow after *Rosa* as she had always done. Slowly, the ebb current caught and turned her, spun her round, then turned her once again, and then she drifted, the axe in her bow, and her bow towards the sea. Marret splashed ashore and came to stand by Steven. Together, they watched the tender float away into the mist, towards the deep dark waters of the bay.

Jakey's death was in the salty air and the mist. It was in the yelping of the gulls and the restless piping of the redshanks. And it was in the quietness which stayed with them.

Marret looked at Steven, but he did not say anything. His eyes were dark and still a long way in. And Steven held his look.

Jakey had gone, and now they must go.

He watched as Marret picked up his sack from the stile. Marret waved once, then he walked away up river towards the distant bridge. He walked into the mist, the sack on his shoulder, and the last that Steven heard of him was his whistling, low and far away, faint and yet near in the still winter night.

The Topiary
Garden

For Hannah

LIZ RAN. "It's not fair!" she yelled. "It's not fair!" And she dashed from the camp site into the lane.

The shadows of the trees striped her, and between them flashed the gables and chimneys of Carlton Hall with the disc of the sun spinning on the tower like a blazing weathervane. Her chest was bursting with anger and her eyes stung as if they had soap in them.

At last she could not run any further. The lane was too steep. She dropped down onto the grass by the dry-stone wall and huddled there for a long time with the new sketchbook clutched in her hands. Dad shouldn't have laughed! He should have belted Alan! He shouldn't have laughed!

Far down the hill she could hear him calling her name, looking for her. Jackdaws circled the chimneys of the Hall. A skylark drifted down the warm evening sky like the ghost of a parachutist. Dad stopped calling and the quietness was all around her.

She rubbed her stinging eyes until sparks came, but she was too angry to cry. An evening breeze hushed through the trees and the leaf shadows swished over her. The sparks faded from her eyes, and she opened her book. On the inside cover Mrs Metcalf had written in beautiful black letters – PRESENTED TO ELIZABETH JACKSON FOR GOOD WORK IN ART. But on the first white page Alan had drawn a crude sketch of the body of a naked woman, graffiti-style – just a body with no head or arms or legs, in red felt-tip pen.

Underneath, he had scribbled *Nude by Alan Michelangelo Jackson!*

Alan was her elder brother. And the small sketchbook, with its green cover and expensive white paper, was the first thing Liz had ever won in her life. The sparks came back to her eyes. She ripped the page out of the book, screwed it up into a ball and shoved it deep into a crack in the wall. Then, much more carefully, she tried to tear out the ragged edge of paper, which meant she had to take out the back page as well. She screwed that up too. She would not let him spoil her prize.

But even though the pages were clean again, she knew that in some way he had. And she knew that if she did not draw something in the book now, this minute, she never would. It would be spoiled forever, because of what Alan had done, and because Dad had laughed.

She took the new pencil out of her back pocket. With quick angry lines she drew a figure running. Underneath, she wrote: *She went away, far away, and never came back.* In the sky above the running figure she drew three black birds, which were the rooks she could see trailing back to the trees. Now some of the anger was on the page, and less of it was inside her.

Again the breeze swished the leaves of the beech trees, and now the sun had gone down behind the tower of the Hall. The sky was streaked with purple and red.

Putting the sketchbook into the back pocket of her jeans, Liz walked quickly on, away from the ruined pages in the wall, and away from the caravan where they were staying. But she knew she would have to go back sometime.

Only the figure in her book could keep running, far, far, over the hills.

It was getting darker now, and a pale moon, like a white snail shell, had crept up the sky. Where a gate opened off the lane into a field, Liz stopped, leaned on the gate post, and stared down into the valley. The first lights flickered on the camp site. She was waiting for Dad to call her again, so that she could pretend not to hear him.

166

The strangeness of being able to see so far calmed more of the anger from her. At home, in Mill Street, all you could see was the Co-Op and the houses across the road. Here, distant fells smoked and darkened on the horizon. A bat flickered under the branches of the trees, weaving an invisible web. The shadows crept together across the lane, until they were not shadows but a blue darkness. The moon brightened.

Liz saw the white scut of a rabbit's tail as it hopped across the dewy grass. She held her breath to watch. The stillness over the countryside was like a very distant sound.

Suddenly the rabbit fled, zig-zagging back to the cover of the wall, startling her. An instant later she heard the munch of footsteps on the stony lane.

A figure came over the slope, leaning on a stick, with the moon on its hunched shoulder.

Liz suddenly felt a long way from the caravan. She stayed very still.

"Evening, lass." It was the voice of an old woman carrying through the quiet air.

"Hello," answered Liz with relief, as the stranger reached her.

"Red at night," said the old woman, jerking her chin towards the last streaks of pink behind the Hall.

Liz stared at her. It looked more like an old man who was standing there in the dark lane, thin and stooping and leaning on a stick, because the woman was wearing a long brown coat tied at the waist with a bit of rope, a pair of black wellies, and, on her head, a cloth cap, like the old men in Mill Street wore. "Pardon?" said Liz politely.

"Red at night,
Shepherd's delight. Should be a grand day tomorrow."

"Oh," said Liz. "My dad'll be pleased. The trials are tomorrow."

"You're here for that, are you?"

"Yes. Dad's in it." Liz fell into step by the stranger. It would be better walking back under the dark whispering branches of the trees with someone else.

"Do you live here?" she asked after a moment, because it

seemed rather rude to say nothing when you walked next to someone.

The old woman walked very slowly, with her nose pointing at the ground and her thin shoulders up round her ears. "Aye. Down there. Yew Tree Cottage. Opposite the topiary garden." Her voice was dry and rattling. "Sally Beck's the name."

"I'm Liz," said Liz.

They walked in silence for a time, with only the sound of their shoes slowly crunching the stones, and the dull tap of Sally Beck's stick.

Liz knew that really she should hurry back to the camp site. Dad would be getting worried. Serves him right! she thought.

"And what's it like, being young these days?" asked the old woman suddenly, glancing sideways at her from the shadow of her cap.

"I don't know," said Liz, surprised. "I've never been anything else!"

Sally Beck chuckled quietly, and gave her stick an extra tap on the ground. Her coat made a swishing sound round her boots as she walked. And the sound was like her laugh.

"Only," said Liz, thoughtfully chewing the end of her plait, and half speaking to herself, "I wish I was a boy sometimes..."

Sally Beck stopped still. And once more the moon stopped behind her shoulder, blue and bright, and not quite a full circle. "Do you now? Now there's a funny thing. I was a boy once upon a time – oh yes, yes I was."

"A boy!" said Liz, staring at her.

"Liz! Lizzy!" her dad was running up the lane towards them. "Where the heck have you been?"

"Come to the Yews. I'll tell you," said Sally Beck. "If you're interested." And she stepped through a gap in the wall and vanished among the trees. Liz gazed after her, until she had gone into the darkness.

"Oh! There you are!" cried Dad. "It was only a joke, Liz. He didn't mean anything."

"What?" said Liz.

"Alan's halfway up Carlton Fell looking for you! He didn't mean to upset you like that." Dad's voice sounded loud in the quiet lane. "You daft tuppence! You might have got lost." He put his arm round Liz's shoulder.

Liz remembered her anger, and shook him off. She walked stiffly ahead of him all the way to the caravan.

"Dad!" said Alan, running towards them across the field. "I can't find her anywhere."

"She's here," said Dad. "Now say you're sorry."

"Sorry, Liz."

"Sod you!" said Liz quietly, as Dad went round the back of the van to turn on the gas-bottle.

"Hoy! It was just a joke!" Alan was four years older than Liz, and too big to hit.

"And not a very funny one at that," said Dad, unzipping the awning.

"You laughed!" cried Liz, accusingly.

"Well, that doesn't mean I thought it was funny," said Dad, lying. "Now give over you two. Don't spoil our weekend, eh?"

The small caravan smelt of the musty canvas and the hot fumes of petrol and oil from Dad's trials-bike which he had put in the awning for safety. Alan was going to sleep next to it, to make sure no one nicked it, or knobbled it, because the first heat of the Carlton Hall Trials Event was tomorrow, and the prize, if Dad won, was a hundred pounds.

Liz dropped down onto her narrow bunk bed, as Dad put a match to the hissing gas-mantles. The light in the caravan suddenly made it pitch black outside.

"Come on, our Lizzy. Put the kettle on," said Dad.

"Shan't."

"Now look what you've done, Alan. You've upset the cook! There goes our bacon butties for the weekend!" Dad laughed, and put the kettle on himself.

"Hey, Liz," said Alan, his leather jacket creaking as he pulled it off. "Did Dad tell you – there's going to be a Fancy

Dress Barbecue on Sunday night." He was smiling at her, trying to make friends again.

Liz shrugged.

"What are you going to go as?" Dad hunted for mugs in the cupboard.

"Dunno yet," said Alan. "Perhaps we could go as Laurel and Hardy." He glanced at Liz. But she wouldn't look at him. "Unless our Lizzy can think of something."

"Sounds like a good idea," said Dad. "And Liz could go as..." he tapped his fingers on the table, trying to think of something. Then he snapped his finger and thumb. "Got it! Liz could go as an artist! You could wear one of my shirts back to front for a smock, and Alan's scarf for a floppy bow tie. And we could make you a pointed beard and a moustache out of cardboard, and one of those palette things."

"Yeh! Great!" said Alan. "You'd look really great!"

Their enthusiasm made Liz feel a bit sick. The sparks came back over her eyes. "Not all artists are men!" she snapped.

"Course they are," said Alan. "Picasso, Michelangelo-er-um-Leonardo da Vinci. Go on then, tell us a woman artist." He was standing in front of her, very cocky, and angry because she wouldn't make friends and forgive him.

Liz opened her mouth. Then shut it again. She was sure there were some women artists, but she could not think of a single name.

The corner of Alan's mouth drew down in a little triumphant grin.

"Sally Beck!" said Liz. It was a lie. It was the first name that came into her head. It was the name of the old woman she had met.

Alan looked at her suspiciously. "Never heard of her."

"Oh, I have," said Dad breezily, stirring the tea. He did not know anything about art or artists. He was just trying to make peace. "Very famous. Isn't she, Liz?"

Liz grinned. "Very, very famous," she said.

Alan shrugged. "I still think Dad's idea was good, anyhow."

170

"Come on, bed, both of you," said Dad, before another squabble broke out.

Liz pulled the curtain round the bunk, so that her bed was like a narrow tent. She crawled into her sleeping bag, with her sketchbook and pencil, and her tin of coloured crayons.

"She went away, far away, and never came back," she read to herself in a whisper, as she shaded in the darkness of the sky and the hill with blue and purple and pink.

Then she turned to the next white page and drew two figures standing under a tree and the moon sitting in the branches like an owl. She thought for a long moment, then she wrote: *And she met a stranger who said Red at night is my delight for I was a boy once upon a time.*

And, writing the words, made a prickly feeling run all along her arms and up to the back of her neck.

"Finished your tea, love?" said Dad, lifting the edge of the curtain.

Liz quickly closed her book.

"Yes, thanks."

"Night, then. Sleep tight, and remember to say a prayer for your mam." Dad had said that every night since Liz was four, when her mam had died.

"Night, Dad," said Liz, as he let the curtain drop. She heard the buzz of Dad's and Alan's voices in the awning, talking about the motorbike and the competition tomorrow. She opened the sketchbook and looked at the two pictures she had drawn.

What Alan had done didn't matter now – at least, not much. Because she had a secret. In her book she was in a strange story, and tomorrow, perhaps, she'd find out what would happen next. Liz was always the figure in her pictures – the small figure with thin arms and legs and two long brown plaits.

PRESENTED TO ELIZABETH JACKSON FOR GOOD WORK. She traced the words proudly with the tip of her finger. "You've got a very distinctive style, Elizabeth," Mrs Metcalf had said when she had given her the prize. "It's a gift. I hope you'll use this sketchbook to develop it over the summer."

Liz smiled to herself. Sally Beck! she thought, and almost laughed out loud. But she made a mental note to ask Mrs Metcalf the names of some real women artists when she got back to school.

She slipped the sketchbook under her pillow and closed her eyes. "Our Father, God bless Dad, and our mam who art in heaven," she murmured dutifully. "And," she added, "make our Alan fall on his face in some mud. Amen."

Then she lay, listening to Dad's voice buzzing on the caravan windows like a brown bee. Somewhere in the moon-blue gardens of Carlton Hall an owl hooted. She fell asleep, thinking of the strange thing the old woman had said.

2

"THAT LAD in the white caravan fancies you, Liz," said Alan, next morning, grinning at her over his bacon butty.

"Shut up," said Liz, turning her own bacon over in the frying pan with a fork. Alan was always saying stupid things like that, trying to embarrass her.

"Hoy,Dad!" said Alan, still grinning, as Dad came in from the awning wiping his hands on an oily rag. "That lad fancies our Liz. He's been watching her ever since she went to the tap."

Dad glanced out of the caravan window. "Well, he isn't watching her now. He's watching that idiot Johnson showing off on his bike." A black line appeared between Dad's eyebrows. He shoved the rag into his pocket and strode back out of the van as a motorbike roared past the awning.

"Can't you blooming read!" They heard him yell. "Hoy! Johnson! I'm talking to you!"

There was a sign at the gate of the field which read: *No bikes to be ridden on the camp site!* That was the rule Carlton Hall had imposed when they rented the field for the competitors to use. The motorbike puttered to a stop, and a moment later Dad came back in, making the caravan rock.

"Idiot! It only takes one to spoil it for the rest of us."

"What did he say?" Alan poured a dollop of tomato sauce onto his bread.

"Nothing I'd repeat before a lady," said Dad, and smiled at Liz. "Anyhow, I told him the marshals would disqualify anyone who broke the rule. That stopped him."

Alan twisted round on the bunk so that he could look out of the window. "Look at him! Showing off in his fancy leathers – just like a big wet girl!"

Liz glared at the bacon which was still spitting in the pan. "Shut up!" she said.

"Now what's the matter?" Dad pulled on his black boot. He glanced up at her.

"Him! Saying that!"

"Saying what?" said Alan, blinking at her.

"Saying that about him showing off like a . . ."

"That's enough! I've just about had enough of you two squabbling!" said Dad, stamping his foot into the boot and yanking up the zip. He held out his hand. His fingernails were black-rimmed with oil. "The palm of this hand is getting very itchy. Very, very itchy. Understand?"

Alan shrugged and glared at Liz. Liz scowled and let the bacon burn. "It isn't fair," she muttered under her breath.

"Anyhow," said Alan. "It's just a saying. It doesn't mean anything."

"Yes, it does!"

"Lii-iiz!" Dad hissed her name, warningly.

"It isn't fair," said Liz again. And went to eat her bacon out on the grass. Alan was always saying insulting, stupid things about girls, but no one apart from her seemed to notice.

It was going to be a warm day – already the sun was high in the sky. The field was like a fairground. There were glittering motorbikes by every caravan, and trucks and trailers. Lines of chequered red and white flags were strung from poles by the gate, and between the poles was a big cloth banner: CARLTON HALL TRIALS EVENT SAT JULY 25TH – SUN JULY 26TH – and in smaller letters underneath:

173

Sponsored by Stoughton's Pale Ale. Clumps of men and boys in bright leathers or black leather jackets flashing with badges, stood round the bikes. The smell of cooking bacon mingled with the smell of petrol across the field. A group of little kids played round the tap near the wall, yelling and splashing up a glittering spray of water.

Through the trees across the road the old chimneys and gables stood darkly, indifferent to all of it. While up on Carlton Fell, where the trials were to take place, a motorbike buzzed like a chain saw.

Liz looked round for someone to make friends with, but she couldn't even see another girl, apart from the little child by the tap, and an older girl who didn't count because her boyfriend had his arm round her shoulder and was kissing her ear. The fringe on the sleeve of his leather jacket hung down her back.

Alan came out of the awning, wheeling Dad's bike. She could tell by the look on his face that he was pretending it belonged to him. And he was wearing an old pair of Dad's motorbike boots. The buckles jinked like spurs.

"Nice bike," said the lad from the white caravan, sauntering across.

"Not bad," said Alan, dead casual, and swung himself astride it. He pretended to be doing something with the throttle.

"Won anything?"

Liz saw Alan hesitate.

"It's me dad's actually," he had to admit, seeing her watching him.

The lad crouched to inspect the silver intestines of the engine. "Oh, I thought it was yours."

Alan smiled, pressing his lips together, very pleased. "I ride it sometimes," he said.

Liz stared at the grass between her sandals, plucked an aimless handful and tossed it away. That's what it would be like all day, she thought. Alan and Dad talking to other competitors about pistons and points and what sort of tyre tread was best, while she'd wander round, until at some point she'd find herself with the wives and girlfriends, making sandwiches and coffee for the marshals, or looking after the little kids. It wasn't much of a way to spend your summer holiday – but that was how they had spent it ever since she could remember. Trials and scrambles and races, year after year.

Alan and the other lad had gone off together to look at another bike. Dad ducked out of the awning, looking like a cross between a diver and a spaceman in his red and black leathers. He grinned at her.

"Going to draw a picture of your old dad on his metal donkey?" he said, coming to sit by her on the grass. His leathers creaked round his knees and elbows.

"I don't like drawing bikes," said Liz. But she thought he looked handsome in his gear, and quite young for a dad. Some of the men looked like the Michelin-tyre man in theirs.

Dad's grin slipped away, and he looked at her thoughtfully. "It's not much fun for you any more, is it Liz?"

Liz plucked another handful of grass.

"It wasn't so bad when you were little like them." He looked at the gaggle of small kids who were stamping through the puddle they had made.

"It's alright," said Liz. But it wasn't really. "Do I have to come up to the fell?" She wanted to go and find the old woman.

"Don't you want to watch me win?"

"Yes. But . . ." She felt mean.

"Well," said Dad. "I suppose you're old enough to be sensible. But don't go far from the camp site."

"I thought I could go and look at the Hall, or something."

"I'll leave you a key for the van – make sure you lock up properly though."

Alan and his new friend came over to them. "Dad, can I go up the fell with Mike and his brother?"

Mike was carrying two helmets by their straps.

"Aye, alright. But don't you go messing about." Dad got to his feet, and tossed Liz the spare caravan key. "I want you both back here for tea – and Lizzy, don't go talking to any strange men."

"They'd have to be strange to talk to our Lizzy!" cried Alan.

Liz put her tongue out at him as far as it would go.

Even in the wood Liz could still hear the intermittent growl of the trials-bikes up on the fell. Now the field next to the camp site was full of cars, and a policeman was standing in the lane, wearing white gloves to direct the traffic and the spectators.

Just for a moment Liz thought about turning back. Sometimes it was good to be among the crowd, knowing your dad was in the competition. It gave you a sort of superior feeling. But she could feel the hard edges of her sketchbook in her pocket, and she knew that today she wanted to be in a story of her own – and not be a spectator on the edge of Dad's and Alan's adventures.

Among the trees the light was green and cool like water, and full of the peppery scents of ferns and brambles. Birds twittered drowsily, making the wood seem very still. She found a path which ran at the foot of a high stone wall, beyond which, she guessed, would lie the gardens of the Hall.

There was something secret about being in the green leafy stillness between the wood and the wall. It was a place for imagining things. But the only trouble was, the harder she tried to pretend something was about to happen, the less certain she became that she really had met the old woman last night in the lane who had said such a strange thing.

Stopping in a patch of sunlight, she took out her book and looked again at the picture she had drawn. 'I was a boy once upon a time.' It sounded a bit daft – and besides, it didn't seem very likely. She chewed thoughtfully at the end of one of her plaits, then flicked it back over her shoulder.

The wall led her round to the front of the Hall where there were a pair of tall wrought-iron gates with gold-tipped spikes. One of the gates stood open, and on the other was a sign: CARLTON HALL. GARDENS OPEN TO THE PUBLIC APRIL–OCTOBER. CHILDREN MUST BE ACCOMPANIED BY AN ADULT.

Beyond the gates was the strangest garden Liz had ever seen – all hedges and yew trees cut into cones and mushrooms, spires and pyramids, like shapes carved out of green pumice stone. Behind them was the Hall itself, grey and formal as a church. One or two couples strolled among the dense green hedges and a man stood with his back to her taking a photograph of a bush clipped to look like a peacock.

Liz decided to ignore the sign – if anyone asked, she'd pretend to be looking for her dad. She slipped through the open gate into the quietness of the garden.

She passed through an archway in a tall green wall. Another plaque was set in the gravel. 'The topiary garden,' she read, 'was created in 1851 by Sir Randolph Chadwick for the pleasure of his wife.'

The green battlements enclosed a secret path, over which loomed the black shapes of the topiary against the bright sky. It was like being among huge chessmen, Liz thought, as she walked slowly among the clipped bushes and trees. She came to a place in the heart of the topiary garden where there was a small, perfectly round lawn, upon which stood a marble statue of a nude woman. Her arms were broken off just above the elbow. And all round her stood black yews like newel posts, like pawns guarding the queen.

The stillness was eerie.

Liz took her pencils and sketchbook from her pocket and sat on the edge of the lawn. She glanced round to make sure no one was looking, then began to draw the statue.

It was difficult, and when she had finished there was something sinister about her picture. It was there in the garden, but it fell like a shadow across the page. The statue looked almost alive – without thinking, Liz had given her arms and hands – and the chessmen weren't guarding her. They were keeping her in, like a pale prisoner.

She drew two figures peering at the statue from behind one of them, and that made the picture even more sinister. The prickly feeling came back along her arms as beneath the drawing she wrote some words. Now the story she was making held a meaning, like a riddle.

"The stranger took her to the topiary garden and showed her a woman turned to stone," she read aloud, very quietly.

"Aye, that's just about the sum of it," said a dry voice and a real shadow fell across the page.

Liz jumped and scrambled to her feet.

It was Sally Beck, still in her coat and wellingtons, smiling at her. She looked even older than she had done the night before. Beneath her cloth cap, her face was like a crumpled brown paper bag.

"I was looking for me dad!" said Liz.

"Were you heck-as-like!" said the old woman, and chuckled. "You come sneaking in that gate like a fox into a hen-coop!"

"Well, I only wanted to see."

"You writing a story?" The old woman jerked her chin towards the sketch-pad.

"I was just drawing a picture. I wasn't doing no harm."

"Any fool can see that," said Sally Beck. "You want a cup of tea?"

Liz nodded. "Yes, please."

"Grand. I just fancied a good natter. And I'll tell you something for nothing, lass, you look a sight more cheerful than you did last night."

"I was a bit fed up then," said Liz, as she walked slowly along with the old woman.

"Just reminded me of meself, you did. Leaning on that gate, scowling at the world.'Sally,' I says to meself when I saw you,'there's another Jack Beck if ever I saw one.'"

They went round the side of the Hall, through a gate, and into a wilder rougher part of the garden where there was a big vegetable patch, a long greenhouse, and a small wooden shed.

"They always leave me a tin of tea in the shed," said Sally Beck. "Like leaving a saucer of milk for an old cat."

"Do you work here, then?" asked Liz, as the old woman unlocked the shed door.

"Work here! I'll have you know – I was head gardener, me lass! Head of all this!" She swept her arm in a wide bony gesture across the hall and its grounds. "Aye, yes, I was. It's too much for me now. I'm ninety-one, you know." She laughed and all the wrinkles of her face trembled. "Ninety-one! Yes. Yes, I am." Then she stopped laughing and looked at the key in her lumpy hand. Her fingers were like a bunch of twisted knobbly sticks. "Ninety-one," she said quietly. "Who would credit it?"

"That means," said Liz, reckoning it up, "That you'll be a hundred in nine years!" She'd never met anyone that old.

Sally Beck shook her head. "Pushing up daisies, more like." She stooped into the shed and fetched out a flask and a stained white mug. "You'll have to have yours out o't lid," she said. Then she lowered herself down onto a bench in the shade. "You pour it, lass. Me hands is all trembles."

Liz did as she asked. It wasn't like being with a stranger at all. She knew that was partly because she had drawn the old woman twice in her book, and although the drawings were not realistic like photographs, anyone who looked at them would have been able to recognise Sally Beck, from the stick and the cap, and the sharp humpy shoulders.

"Eh," sighed the old woman as Liz handed her the mug. "It's not all a bed of roses."

"What isn't?"

"Being ninety-one. Head gets full of cobwebs – just like this old shed. It's your faculties, see. Full of cobwebs and rusty old things. Aye, it's your faculties. They get rusty after a life-time int' rain. . ." She sucked her tea noisily from the rim of the mug, "and all the folks that were your friends and your foes are all dead and done, until there's only theesen." Sally Beck's voice was like the rattle of leaves along a gravel path. "I wasn't always old like this, lass. But there's nobbut me and Him minds the time when I looked like you."

They were silent for a long moment. The hot sky rippled like silk above the trees, and the faint roar of the motorbikes on the fell was like the tearing of cotton.

Liz said, "It sounds a bit lonely."

"Lonely?" Sally Beck nodded. Her neck wobbled under

her chin. "Aye, it's lonely. Sometimes. Makes you feel like a ghost sometimes..."

"You looked a bit like a ghost last night." Liz grinned, remembering the footsteps on the quiet lane.

"Give you a fright, did I?"

"Just for a minute," said Liz. Then she did something she rarely did. She pulled out her sketchbook and opened it for Sally Beck to see. "I drew you."

"Hold on." The old woman fumbled in her pocket for a pair of spectacles. She took the sketchbook and held it close to her face. She did not say anything. After a time she turned the page and looked at the other two drawings. "You did these, lass?" Round her mouth the lines trembled like dusty cobwebs.

Liz nodded. She watched the old woman's lips move silently as she read the words to herself. The quiet of the garden surged round them, and through the archway in the hedge Liz could see the shadow of the statue lying like a sundial across the lawn.

"That's a strange story you're writing," said Sally Beck at last.

"Oh," said Liz. Her face felt hot. "It's not really a proper story..."

Sally Beck unhooked the spectacles from her ears and looked at Liz from under the shadow of her cap. "Now, this here," she pointed to the first picture Liz had drawn. "This might have been Jack Beck. That's to say, me. Ont' day I became Jack Beck." The way she said it, it sounded more like the beginning of an argument than the beginning of a story.

"Did you really mean it, then? About you being a boy?" Liz stared at her.

"Certainly! Certainly, I did. It's God's honest truth I'm telling you, me lass!" said Sally Beck indignantly, "Eh, and by the road, it isn't 'Red at night is my delight' – it's 'shepherd's delight.'"

"I know. But I liked it better my way," Liz said.

"Do you want me to tell you this story or don't you?"

"Yes!"

"Well, stop interrupting us then. And pour us the rest of me tea."

3

SALLY RAN. The shadows of the houses striped her and between the terraces flashed the early morning sun. 'Clack-clack-clack' went her clogs on the cobbles and the echo of them rang from the walls of Holyroyd Mill.

"I can hear that sound now, ringing in me ears, like someone was after me."

'Clack-clack-clack' through the empty streets, scattering the sparrows and jackdaws from their pickings on the road. But already she could hear the 'clitter-clat, clitter-clat' of the other clogs as all through the streets of Holyroyd, men and women made their way from the houses to the cotton mill.

It was the morning after her twelfth birthday, and she had run away. And by the time Saint Peter's struck six o'clock on that July morning Sally Beck was already on top of Holyroyd Hill with the bundle of stolen clothes and a loaf of bread clutched to her chest.

"'If tha'll not get in service, tha'll get int' mill till tha's wed an' ah can wash me hands o' thee, Sally Beck – now get me supper.' That's what me Dad said on me twelfth birthday. That's all the present I got."

Sally kept running until the mill chimney was hidden by the rise of the moor. Then she took off her skirt and her apron and her shawl and shoved them into a hole in the bottom of a dry-stone wall. It felt like the first time her arms and legs had ever seen the sun. She unrolled the bundle of clothes she had stolen off the end of the bed she shared with her brother Jack and her sister Alice. They were Jack's clothes she had pinched, and she put them on – trousers, and a shirt cut down from an old one of her dad's, brown waistcoat and white muffler. With a knife she had stolen from the kitchen, she sawed off her plaits, "And they lay like two brown snakes on the ground."

Up on the moors the wind blew cold on her bare neck. She pulled her brother's cap onto her head. Then, with the loaf of bread tucked in her shirt, she walked off over the moor, following green sheep paths through the heather, looking for a road. She was up on the moors for three days, without seeing another soul, and at night she slept by the walls. She was twelve. "I was that hungry I tried to eat some grass, but when I picked a blade it left two streaks down me finger and thumb – because of the soot from the chimney of Holyroyd Mill, and all t'other mills in the valleys round."

"And at night I was that frit – I thought sheep would grow long teeth in the dark and come and eat me when I slept!"

Three days after she had run away, Sally met a man sitting by a little fire at the side of a white moorland road. Next to him was a cart, and a horse picketed out on a long rope. He was cooking some eggs in a tin over his fire, and in his hand he held a piece of cheese, and he was eating lumps of the cheese off the blade of his knife. But he never cut his tongue.

"I can't rightly remember what he said, that man. I come out of the heather and just stood staring at the cheese, and he give us some in the end. But he must have asked me name, because I told him me name was Jack Beck – that was me brother whose clothes I had on."

Sally was thin – she had always been thin. But after three days sleeping rough on the moor, she was thinner than ever. And the man did not guess that the boy who leaned against his cartwheel was really a girl.

In the back of the cart were slabs of grey stone settled in straw. They didn't have any words carved on them, but Sally knew at once what they were. She had seen stones like that in Saint Peter's churchyard. And when she sat on one of them in the jolting cart, she could not decide whether it was better or worse sitting on a grave-stone that had no name on it. A stone without a name was somebody's future, while any stone with a name on it was somebody's past.

The carter took her over the Pennines. He was a brown sour-faced man with a big black moustache. He didn't speak much – except to his horse. But he was kind in a rough way – sharing his meals. And it was him who taught her the name of her first flower – Death Come Quickly. "Herb Robert, most folks call it now – a little pink thing with ferny leaves."

She had banged her arm on the side of the cart one morning, and he picked it and rubbed it on the bruise.

"That's a fine finicky hand for a lad, Jack," he said, holding her wrist.

"I've been badly," said Sally, snatching her hand away.

The man looked at her for a long time, chewing his moustache thoughtfully. Then he shrugged.

Sally was sure he had guessed. He never said a word. But that night he put his jacket over her to keep her warm, and in the morning he went over a wall to relieve himself, instead of going against the hub of the cartwheel as he had done before.

Late that afternoon they came down off the moors, onto a lane beneath the whispering branches of tall trees. Sally slipped quietly off her grave-stone in the back of the cart. The man did not notice, because he was busy with the horse and the wooden brake, going so steeply downhill. She hid behind the gate post of a field until the very last sound of hooves and cartwheels had faded away.

She had no idea where she was – only that it was a long way from Holyroyd. When she stood up, the first thing she saw was the grey chimneys and gables of a big house among the trees, and the sun sitting on its tower like a blazing weather vane.

"Carlton Hall!" said Liz, sitting up and rubbing her elbow which had gone stiff from leaning.

"Aye. It was. But I didn't know that then. Any road up, who's telling this story? Thee or me?"

"Thee! I mean, you!"

"Well hold your noise, lass. You'll muddle me faculties. Now, where was I?"

"Carlton Hall."

"Oh, aye. Well now, at that time the head gardener was a chap called Samuel Cumpsty."

Sally had been standing with her head pressed between the railings of the wrought-iron gate for a long time before the man noticed her. He was an elderly man with a big stomach and thin legs. He had a face like a turnip, fringed with white side-burns. And he was standing on a pair of wooden steps, clipping away at a green bobbin of a bush, in a garden that looked as if it were made out of green bobbins and spools and newel posts. It was the strangest garden Sally had ever seen, but she could tell the bobbins were really only dense bushes and trees, because green clippings lay scattered all over the gravel path.

At last the man turned round on the steps, sat on them, took a stone from his pocket and began to sharpen the blades of the shears, stroking the stone along the blades with a long hissing whisper. For a time he frowned at the boy at the gate. Then he put the stone back in his waistcoat pocket. "You looking for something, lad?"

"Aye," said Sally Beck. "I'm looking for a job of work."

"And what line of a trade are you in?" said the man as he began clipping at the bush again. "Begging or thieving, I'll wager, by the look on you."

"I am not!" said Sally. The sun was going down behind the grand house, and the shadows of the gate were lying over the lane. "Fetching and carrying – I can do that."

"Oh aye," said the man, without looking round. "And can you say your prayers?"

"Our Father which art in Heaven hallowed be thee name," said Sally, very quickly.

"Fetching and carrying, is it?" The man straightened up and pushed back his cap. "Well, fetch us that broom and carry them clippings to yon pile."

"And that was how I got me first job. As it turns out, his last lad had died of lock-jaw at Easter. Mr Cumpsty, I had to call him, and he called me Jack. And going through those big black gates was like going through the gates of heaven itself."

Sally Beck and Samuel Cumpsty worked until it was dark. Not a leaf or a twig was to be left on the gravel from his clipping, and although he had spread sacks under the bushes, it still took a long time to clear up. The moon was high by the time they had finished. And it was by moonlight that they raked smooth the gravel among the topiary trees.

184

Mr Cumpsty took her back to his cottage and, that night, for the first time in her life, Sally had a bed to herself. And, what's more, she had a mug of ale to put her to sleep.

The next morning he took her to the Hall, and it was there that Sally learned that all the hiring and firing was done by a man called Harrison, who wore white gloves. "He was only a servant to Sir Chadwick like the rest of the staff, but he thought he was God Almighty hisself! I thought he was the Devil – all in black, with a thin nose, and white hands." Even Sam Cumpsty had to take off his cap and hold it in front of him when he talked to that man." Harrison merely glanced at Sally, and wrote the name 'Jack Beck' in a black book.

"It wasn't until four years later that I met the man I was working for – Sir William Chadwick... But I haven't come to that bit yet."

And so Sally became Jack, the gardener's lad, at Carlton Hall.

"And do you know, lass, the thing I remember most – the thing that was me freedom? Aye, daft it'll sound, but me freedom was being able to walk through the garden, with me hands in me pockets, whistling. Whistling! You see, it was like this then – in Holyroyd there was a saying,

'A whistling woman and a crowing hen
Brings bad luck to gentlemen.'

And if a lass was heard whistling, she'd get a clout. But Jack Beck could whistle to his heart's content – long as he was at his job, mind."

"But weren't you scared you'd be found out?" said Liz. The shadow of the statue had crept out of sight across the lawn.

"Scared! I was witless! Witless scared, sometimes. And at night I'd lie in me little bed, listening to Samuel Cumpsty snoring over me head, and an owl moaning in the trees, and I'd think on me brothers and sisters what I'd left. Till thinking made me cry some nights. Aye, that it did. But I wasn't for going back. I'd got something none of me sisters had – a bed I didn't have to share with anyone else; not with a sister, or a babby, or a husband... You'll not understand that, lass..."

"But what about your mam?" said Liz, thoughtfully, "Didn't you miss her?"

"She was past missing," said the old woman. "Her name was on one of them stones in Saint Peter's churchyard when I was eight. There were nine live children in me family when I ran from Holyroyd. And three dead ones. And the last of those dead ones was a little lad who came feet first and kicked himself and me mam to death with the birthing of him."

"Topiary," said Sam Cumpsty, wiping his forehead on his sleeve, "is the Devil's own art!"

"How do you mean, Mr Cumpsty?" asked Sally. She had been at Carlton Hall three years and had still managed to keep her secret – but it was getting harder every day. Cumpsty's Tail, the Hall staff had nick-named the thin lad who spent all his time with the old gardener. But on the whole they thought well enough of Jack. He was hardworking, shy, kept himself to himself, they said.

"Well, you reckon it up, Jack," said Sam, coming down the stepladder. He sat on the edge of the lawn, the shears across his knees. He reached for the jug of cider they had left in the shade and tilted it on his arm to drink. Then he wiped his mouth, and continued, "Eight weeks every year it takes us to clip this lot – two whole months back and front of every summer. By the time you've been here six years – you'll have spent one whole year of your natural born days, clip-clipping these feckless articles!"

He passed the cider jug to Sally.

"I'll tell you something, Jack lad – when you get to my age you get to doing a bit of philosophising."

"What?"

"Thinking, Jack! Thinking! Using what's between your ears for more than keeping your cap on!"

"Oh," said Sally. Her arm ached from wielding the heavy shears. They were working on a yew tree that had been grown and clipped and wired to the shape of an egg-timer. "What have you been thinking, Mr Cumpsty?"

"I've been thinking that topiary's the Devil's own art.

That's what. I've been thinking of all the years of me four-score and ten that I've spent turning what's natural into what's unnatural, just for the pleasing of a gentleman's eye... Look at that yew – it should be a fine big churchyard tree by now. But oh no – our Sir William wants a wasp-waist of a useless article!"

Sally eyed their work. "It's like putting a tree in corsets," she said thoughtfully.

Sam Cumpsty laughed and slapped his knee. "Aye! It is that, Jack! Putting Mother Nature into corsets and stays – that's our job in the topiary garden. And all so that Sir William can glance up from his table and see her displayed for his pleasure!"

"Is that why they've put Liddy in corsets, do you reckon, Mr Cumpsty?" said Sally, as they walked back across the gravel path. Liddy was a maid at the Hall – a girl of about Sally's own age. And a week ago she had changed shape, from being soft and plump to being an egg-timer.

Sam laughed again. "Aye, it's much the same thing." Then he frowned. "Here, don't you go making fresh with young Liddy, Jack."

"Oh, I shan't do that, Mr Cumpsty," said Sally, and blushed for reasons that Samuel Cumpsty couldn't even have guessed.

Seeing Jack with a scarlet face, Sam smiled. "Aye, you're a good lad. Now hand us them shears."

"I thought to meself – there's more topiary going on in this garden than you've mind of, Samuel Cumpsty!"

It wasn't just Liddy up at the Hall who was changing shape. Sally was as well. And it was getting harder to disguise the fact. She felt safe enough in the garden, and in her small room at Sam's cottage which she shared with the garden-forks and spades and a terrier called Nelson. But the garden wasn't the only place she and Sam worked. Once a fortnight they were lent to the church down at Carlton Beck, to scythe the grass and trim the graves, and even to dig graves sometimes if the vicar's man was ill.

And, during the hay-making and the harvest they were expected to give a hand on the estate's farms.

"You see, lass, it wasn't that I wanted to be a boy in me nature or me body – I just wanted to be Sally Beck. Not Jack. But Sally Beck with Jack's freedom – do you follow? But I was getting so as I had to tie a bit of cotton rag tightly round me chest to stop them showing through me shirt and waist-coat. And once a month it was harder still. . . I knew in me bones that it couldn't go on. Those three years had been the happiest of me life. But I knew in me bones it was coming to an end – or to put it more basic, I knew in me hips and me bosom."

While the lads on the farms were growing their first fluffy beards, and their voices were going cracked high and low, "like the mouse-eaten bellows on the organ at Carlton Beck," Cumpsty's Tail was smooth-faced and, not so much thin, as willowy.

"I took some teasing that summer, lass, I can tell you. And I was that fond of old Sam, and that frit on him finding out, that I often lay awake all night, thinking I should run away again. And the worse teasing of all was from that Liddy."

Every morning Sally had to go to the Hall kitchen to take an order from Mrs Baxter, the cook, for the vegetables she wanted for the day. Sam and Jack Beck grew most of the vegetables in a walled garden behind the Hall – there was even a peach tree growing against a south-facing wall, that was Mr Cumpsty's pride and joy.

"'Now then, Jack, I want a couple of them nice onions, and some carrots, and I'll have a big basket of strawberries. Nice ones mind – his Lordship's got guests this evening. Oh, and what else? Aye, some bay-leaves and some rosemary for the lamb.' And Mrs Baxter would give me a big wicker basket, and, sometimes an oat cake or a bit of fruit cake – whatever she was baking."

But Liddy was often there as well, dressed in her black uniform and white collar, trying to pinch Jack's cap as he went through the door, or singing softly under her breath,

"What ails
Cumpsty's Tail
Can't grow a beard
So I've heard!"

"I died a thousand deaths going in that kitchen, lass. I had this feeling that Liddy would find me out – which she did in the end, in a manner of speaking... Eh, poor Liddy..."

"What happened?" said Liz. The shadow of the Hall had crept over them. And now the garden was very still. All the visitors had left, and the sound of motorbikes had died away to a summer evening's silence.

The old woman was staring at the ground, seeing something there that Liz could not see, but she could imagine. Another summer, over seventy years ago. The last summer of Jack Beck's whistling, with his hands in his pockets, in the topiary garden.

One Friday in late July a message came from the sexton at Carlton Beck. There was a grave to be dug for a young lad who had died on a local farm, gored by a bull. And the regular grave-digger was ill.

Samuel Cumpsty had woken that morning with a bad stomach, and he grumbled all the way to the churchyard, which was a three mile walk, although his stomach grumbled louder.

It was a hot day, and their boots were covered with dust by the time they got there. The grave was to be dug by the churchyard wall, far from the cool shadow of the black yew trees which grew by the lych-gate. The ground was stony and parched hard.

First they had to cut off the turfs which would be put back over the grave after the lad was buried. Sally did that, cutting neat squares with the blade of her shovel, and stacking the turf by the wall. But that was the easy part.

Then came the picking and the shovelling.

"Here," groaned Sam, at last. "You dig it Jack, and I'll lie in it."

"Eh, Mr Cumpsty," said Sally, leaning on her spade, up to her waist in the hole. "Don't say that!" The sweat was running down her back and her ribs. More than anything in the world at that moment, she wanted to take off her shirt. But she daren't even take off her waistcoat.

"I'll tell you, Jack," said Sam Cumpsty, dabbing at his face with his handkerchief. "If I dig yon grave, it'll be me last. And if that blighter of a grave-digger was here, I'd belt him over the head with me shovel – then he'd know what it was like to feel badly! I'm telling you, lad! If that blighter's ill today it'll be because he's had a jug too many at the Carlton Arms!"

Sally grinned. But then she looked at old Sam. His face was like melting butter in the hot sun, " ...and he was holding himself stiff, like. All crooked. He was in no state for digging a grave – save his own. And it scared me."

"Mr Cumpsty," said Sally "you get on back to the cottage. I can finish up here. I've done it before. I promise – it'll be the tidiest bit of digging this side of Carlton Fell."

"I've mind to take your advice, lad," said Sam.

"Where there's a mind there's a will, Mr Cumpsty. I'll dig it right, don't you fret."

Sam nodded. He put his jacket back on, and pulled his cap out of his pocket to cover his balding head from the sun.

"You're a grand lad," he said. "And that poor soul you're digging grave for was same age as you. Think on. The vicar'll have a sermon out of your digging, I warrant."

Then Sally was left alone in the graveyard, among the urns and white angels of the gentry and farmers, and the grey stones which cast their shadows over the green mounds of poorer folk.

It took her all afternoon to dig that hole. Until she was stood at the bottom, with the planks of wood shoring the sides to stop them caving in on her and burying her alive. She was fifteen, rising sixteen, and above her was a hot blue rectangle of sky. "I was that tired when it was done – I just lay down on the cool earth at the bottom of the grave. I pulled me cap over me eyes, and the next thing was – I was fast asleep."

When Sally woke, the moon was up. A sickle moon, above the squat tower of the church. For a second she could not remember where she was. She got stiffly to her feet and was about to climb out of the grave, when she heard a whisper and a giggle.

She stopped still, listening, afraid. But these weren't ghosts she was hearing. She recognised the laugh and the giggle – it was Liddy, the maid from the Hall. And, a moment later, she recognised the other voice – it was a labourer on one of the estate's farms. "Handsome as the Devil, he was. And married, with two little children and another one coming."

"I love you, Liddy," she heard him murmur. "Be kind to me, lass. Oh, be kind to me . . ."

Sally contemplated jumping out of the grave and giving them both a scare. But, instead, she crawled quietly out of the hole. Liddy and the labourer were not in the graveyard at all, but in the field over the wall. And now there were no voices, but sighs and gasps.

As quietly as she could, Sally collected up the shovels and the pick, and crept away through the grave-stones. Once she was out on the lane, she ran.

When she got back to the cottage, Sam was sitting in a chair outside the door, drinking a glass of sherry with an egg in it, that Mrs Baxter had brought down for him.

"Is it done?" he asked.

"Aye," said Sally. "I've made it neat, and it's all shored up. I fell asleep, Mr Cumpsty."

"Here," said Mrs Baxter, who was standing next to the chair. "Have you seen our Liddy?"

"No," Sally lied. But her voice made it sound like a lie. And both Mrs Baxter and Mr Cumpsty heard.

"Well," said Sam, handing his glass back to the cook. "There's no harm in seeing, is there?"

"That depends," said Mrs Baxter. "That depends."

By October, Liddy had changed shape again. And the labourer, his wife and three small children had gone. They went by night. No one ever saw them again.

It was Harrison who came for Sally. She was up in an apple tree in the orchard, tossing down apples to old Sam.

"Jack Beck?" said Harrison, as if her name wasn't worth

191

the spittle he used in his saying it. "Sir William wants a word with you."

"Me?" Sally swung from a branch and landed in the soft grass.

"Harrison marched me off, as if I was to be hanged. And there was nothing Sam Cumpsty could do but stare, with a basket of apples in his arms."

As they crunched up the gravel path, Harrison never said a word. But Sally knew, before they entered the panelled library, that Jack Beck's time was up. Someone had found out. She wanted the floorboards to open up and swallow her. And yet, also, there was a sense of relief. She had a feeling that she would have to pay for those happy years she had had. But she was ready to pay for them. It was like dying, but it was better than running away.

Sir William Chadwick was smaller than Sally had imagined – only the size of ordinary people, in fact. And older. His wife, Lady Chadwick, had died before Sally had come to Carlton Hall, and his only son lived in the south. Sir William spent a great deal of time in London, and Sally had only seen him once or twice before – standing at the library window, or strolling through the gardens.

"I like to think of my servants as family," he said, and doodled on his blotting paper. Without lifting a hand or saying a word, he somehow sent Harrison away.

"I stood in front of his desk, with me cap in me hands, while he give us this long sermon about family and responsibility and loyalty. I could tell by the look on him that he was not enjoying lecturing me – but I didn't know what he were on about."

"Well, Beck? Speak up. There's no need to be afraid," said Sir William.

Sally just frowned at the polished floor, baffled and scared.

"Of course," said Sir William, looking uncomfortable, "Liddy has been given her notice. The question remains – what are we to do with you, Beck?"

Then, suddenly, it dawned on Sally what this interview was about. Liddy was going to have a baby, and Sir William had been told that Jack Beck was the father of the child! "I just stood gawping at him. I couldn't believe me ears! Whatever possessed Liddy I'll never know – perhaps she was that shamed to admit she'd been with a married man. Or, more like, she wouldn't tell them the name of the man, and Mrs Baxter had remembered that night when I was late home from the churchyard. Any way up, I was in the queerest pickle. I knew I was about to get the sack.

"Sally, I thought to meself, you may as well be hung for a sheep as a lamb!"

Sir William was standing with his back to her, looking out of the library window over the topiary garden. His hands were behind his back, and he was tapping the two fingers of his right hand in the palm of his left.

"It wasn't me!" said Sally.

"I'd rather you didn't lie to me, Beck. It's a deuced bad business as it is."

Sally took a deep breath. "It can't have been me, Sir," she said.

Sir William turned, frowning. "Oh, and why not?"

"Because," said Sally in a whisper. "Me name's not Jack, Sir. It's Sally."

"Pardon?" Sir William stared at her.

"Me name's not really Jack, Sir. It's Sally. And I'm not a lad. I'm a lass."

There was a silence like thunder.

"I was shaking that much, I thought I was going to fall down. And Sir William looked as if he was going to fall down, and all! Any road, to cut a long story short, I was dragged off to the kitchen by Mrs Baxter, and made to take all me clothes off in front of her. I stood on the cold tiles as naked as a nail. And she was that overcome she burst into tears and blew her nose on her apron.

"Then there was that much conflabbing and consternation. They couldn't have been more shocked if Jack Beck had grown wings and flown away!

"Harrison was all for handing me over to the law, for fraud and deception. Well, I was given a skirt belonging to another maid to put on, and I was taken back to Sir William. I was that used to britches, I felt naked dressed like that... Any road, I spent all evening with his lordship – sobbing, I was. And I had to tell him the story of me life." The old woman smiled at Liz.

And Liz was gazing at her, unaware that the shadows in the topiary garden had joined to a blue darkness.

"He let us stay on! I couldn't believe it. But he let us stay on, as a gardener! I wasn't to live at Sam Cumpsty's cottage any more – that wasn't decent now I was a lass! And I wasn't to work in the churchyard or in the fields. Of course there was a right scandal and Harrison tried to make life a torment until the day he died. But Sir William always had a kind word, and so did Mrs Baxter when she come round."

"But what about Samuel Cumpsty?" said Liz.

The old woman shook her head sadly. "He never spoke to me again. It wrung me heart, that did. And he died that winter of this cancer in his stomach. He'd been like a father to Jack... I could still weep when I think on... He was buried down at Carlton Beck, and I always kept his grave nice, with flowers and that.

"They were going to employ a new gardener, but somehow they never got round to it. Then Kaiser's War came on and the whole world changed. By the time that was done, I was back at Sam Cumpsty's cottage as head gardener and Sir William – he was an old man in a bath-chair by then, – often come down the garden for a talk. And when he died, he left it in his will that Sally Beck was to have the cottage to live in for the rest of her days. So here I've stayed.

"Now what do you think of that, me lass?"

Liz shook her head. "Didn't you miss being Jack?"

"Heavens, no!" cried Sally Beck. "Oh, I'd been happy then – but I was far happier being meself for the rest of me days! But I'll tell you something – I've still got Jack Beck's waistcoat and cap, and his leather leggings and boots. I just kept them for sentimentality, I suppose." The old woman held out her hand. "Here, lass. Give us a pull up. I've got stiff with sitting."

Liz jumped to her feet and helped haul her off the bench. It was getting darker.

"You'd better run," said Sally Beck. "They lock the gates at nine."

"Oh heck!" cried Liz. "I was meant to be back for tea-time!" She grabbed her sketchbook. "Thanks for telling me the story! I'll come and see you tomorrow."

"Aye, if you've a mind. I'm mostly in the garden, or at me cottage. Good-night, lass."

"Good-night!" cried Liz, and dashed away through the eerie shapes of the topiary trees.

4

DAD WAS FURIOUS. "I've got half the camp site looking for you!" It was a bit of an exaggeration.

"I'm sorry. I never noticed the time."

"Well, where the heck were you?"

"I was at the Hall, talking to the gardener."

"What did I tell you about talking to strange men! I might as well talk to a brick wall!"

"It wasn't a man. It was a woman, called Sally Beck. I am sorry, Dad. Honest, I am."

Dad sighed. "Well, at least you're safe. Now get in the caravan."

Shortly afterwards, Alan and his friend, Mike, came back.

"She's here," said Dad. "Now come on, let's get some supper on. My stomach thinks my throat's been slit!"

Soon, the smell of frying beefburgers and onions filled the caravan. Liz sat by the window, watching Dad cook, but she was thinking about Jack Beck.

"Well, aren't you going to ask?" said Dad.

"Ask what?" said Liz.

"If I won."

"Oh! Did you?"

"No. But I came third!" Dad grinned, very pleased with

himself, and forgetting that he was supposed to be angry with her.

"Great! Does that mean you win a prize?"

"No, but it means I qualify for tomorrow's event, and I'm in with a good chance. Do you want onions on your beef-burger?"

"Yes, please."

Dad passed Alan and Mike a plate each. They were out in the awning, sharing a can of beer. Then he came and sat opposite Liz. "Have you thought any more about the fancy dress, Lizzy?"

Liz shook her head. She had forgotten all about it.

"Dad?" said Liz, as she poured herself a mug of tea. "You know when I said I'd been talking to the gardener – why did you think I meant a man?"

"I don't rightly know. It's just what you expect, I suppose..." Dad remembered he was angry again. "Now you listen to me, our Lizzy. When I say tea-time, I mean tea-time!"

"Yes, Dad."

Liz had a nightmare. She was in the topiary garden but now all the trees and bushes were really women, like the statue on the lawn. Green women, rooted to the soil.

And a man with a thin nose and white gloves was walking among them, snipping off their arms with a huge pair of shears. He came towards Liz, and she suddenly realised that she was a topiary woman as well. 'S-nap! Ss-nap!' went his shears as he came at her.

And Liz jerked awake. Her face was wet with sweat, and the sleeping bag was tied in a knot round her legs. Outside, it was light. She could hear Dad breathing softly at the other end of the caravan. And the awning was flapping in the cool dawn breeze. That was the sound she had heard in her dream.

She straightened the sleeping-bag and lay back down, but she could not get back to sleep. The dream was like a picture in her mind.

Soon it would be morning. It was getting lighter all the

time. Dad turned onto his back and started to snore quietly in the back of his throat.

At last she got her sketch-book and pencils from the end of the bunk, and she tried to put the picture of her dream down on the page, until concentrating on the drawing made the fear go away. It was a weird picture – the topiary women were roughly sketched in, with long black shadows lying at their feet. And, for some reason, even those that had had their arms cut off still had them in their shadows.

In the centre of the picture she drew a man. He was thin, all dressed in black, wielding a huge pair of scissors, almost as big as himself. They were meant to be shears, but they looked more like scissors, and that made the picture weirder still. She thought he looked like the Devil, so she drew two tiny horns sticking out of his head, – but she didn't give him a tail.

Under the picture, she wrote *Topiary is the Devil's own art* which is what Samuel Cumpsty had said to Jack Beck.

Yawning, she began to colour in the sky, and, with her cheek resting on the page, she fell back to sleep.

Liz ran through the open gate and into the black shadows of the topiary trees. Then she stopped, disconcerted. It gave her an odd feeling being among the clipped bushes, so soon after her dream. It was like walking out of one room into another, and finding the same person seated in both.

On her wrist she was wearing Dad's watch. "Back at six," he had said, "or you'll miss the barbecue." She had still been in her sleeping bag when he and Alan set off up the fell, for the last trials' event of the weekend. They would be leaving tomorrow morning, early, because Dad had to be at work at the garage by nine.

She found the old woman sitting on the bench by the shed. At her feet was a big wicker basket containing a lumpy brown paper parcel, a bunch of radishes and a lettuce.

"Now then," said Sally Beck, "I've brought something to show you."

"I've got something to show you as well," said Liz, pulling her sketchbook out of her pocket.

Sally Beck chuckled. "You first then."

"I had a bad dream about the garden last night," said Liz, pulling her sketch-book out of her pocket. "Look, that's a picture of it."

The old woman put on her spectacles. "It looks like that devil, Harrison! It must have been a blooming bad dream!"

"That's who it's meant to be, I think."

"Here! I hope you're not going to hold me responsible for your dreams, lass!"

Liz laughed. "I shan't," she said. But she had a feeling that she would visit the topiary garden again in nights to come.

"I'm pleased to hear it," said Sally Beck. "Want a radish?"

"No, thanks. I've just had my dinner." Dad had left her a plate of sandwiches.

"Now then. You have a look in there." The old woman poked the brown paper parcel with the end of her stick.

Liz sat on the grass at her feet and untied the string, but she had already guessed what it contained. There was a strong smell of moth-balls.

Inside, there were a pair of brown boots, a cloth cap, a green waistcoat, and two pieces of leather fringed with buckles.

"Now then," said Sally Beck. "They're what you call 'leggings'. I give 'em a bit of a rub with lard this morning, to bring up the shine."

"Lard?"

"Aye. By rights it should be pig fat dubbin. Here, try them on. First put on the boots. Well, go on! They might not fit you, mind."

Reluctantly, Liz pulled off her sandals and tried on the boots. They were stiff and hard. The leather had cracked in places, but they were big enough. The eye-holes were newly threaded with pieces of string. She had a picture in her mind of Jack Beck lying at the bottom of the grave, looking up at the rectangle of twilight, hearing whispers and giggles. It was like putting on a dead person's clothes.

"Now, wrap leggings round your calf. No, you daft youth! T'other way up! Aye, that's right. Now, do up the buckles."

The buckles were rusty and stiff. They nipped her fingers, but at last she stood and looked down at her old-fashioned feet. "They're a bit like Dad's motorbike boots," she said. She looked at the waistcoat. It was faded, and there was a brown stain down the green satin back.

She did not want to put it on. She was afraid of something, but she wasn't sure what. Something daft – a daft fear that the clothes might whisk her back in time, like in a story, to a life of having to pretend to be something you were not. Of only being able to feel free by hiding what you really were with a tightly bound cotton rag and a waistcoat.

There was something daft and devilish about Sally Beck's story. Not in what she had done, which was brave, but in the fact that she had to do it at all.

But the old woman was smiling at her, wanting to see how she would look.

Liz put on the cap.

"No, pull it back. Here, let me do it." With her twiggy fingers she yanked the cloth cap on Liz's head. Then she took it off again. "Stick your plaits on your head."

Liz held up her hair, and Sally Beck pushed the cap firmly back.

Liz's ears felt naked, and her neck felt bare. She slipped the waistcoat over her T-shirt.

"Horn, them buttons," said the old woman as Liz fastened them. "Mrs Baxter used to buy them off this tinker chap..." She fell silent. She looked at Liz out of the dry crinkles of her face. Her own cap cast a black shadow across her eyes. Then she pulled a clean white handkerchief from her coat pocket. Liz leaned forward and the old woman knotted it round her neck.

They were both silent.

At last Sally Beck said, very quietly, "I was thinner and plainer than you, lass."

The silence went on.

"And I had two shirts – one for working, and one for best. And they both had buttons carved out of sea shells. Shirts you had to pull on over your head... Nearest I ever got to the sea, them little white buttons..."

Somewhere in the topiary garden a thrush was singing. And a jackdaw croaked on the tower of Carlton Hall with a sound like, 'Tjack! Jack!' With a sound like a black laugh.

Liz did not need a mirror. She knew what the old woman was seeing from her shadowed eyes.

Funny, thought Liz. My name's Jackson. Jack's son... I wonder why there isn't a Jackdaughter?

She shook her head. It was like trying to wake up. Then she took off the cap. And the waistcoat and the boots and the leggings. She put them back in the paper, and tied up the parcel with string.

The old woman watched her. Her face was so dry and withered, Liz could not read her expression, any more than you could guess what a tree stump was thinking. But then she smiled, and nodded slowly.

Liz said, "Did you never go back to Holyroyd?"

"No," said Sally Beck. "I never did. I never saw me sisters or me brothers again. But I can guess where they'll be now. Under grey stones, lass. Under grey stones."

"Ninety-one..." said Liz, looking at her.

"Aye," said Sally Beck. "We're a long living breed us women." She laughed very softly. "Gives us a chance to see the world change, lass. Yes. Yes, it does."

The bonfires for the barbecue were already glowing on the camp site field when Liz got back. The flames looked pale and small against the bright evening sky.

Dad and Alan were in the awning, laughing and writing signs saying 'Laurel' and 'Hardy' to hang round their necks, because you could not really tell who they were meant to be from the clothes they had on.

"Hello, our Lizzy!" said Dad. "Guess who came second?"

"Only the man himself!" said Alan, and pointed his finger at Dad's ear.

"That's great!" said Liz.

"Well, what are you going as?" Dad stuffed a cushion up his shirt to make him look fatter.

"Oh..." She had forgotten all about the Fancy Dress. She

frowned and glanced round the camp site. There were laughs and shouts from the other caravans. A cowboy and a pirate were strolling over to the fire.

"Well?" said Dad.

A black bird flew across the pale rising moon, heading for the chimneys of Carlton Hall.

'Tjack! Jack!'

"Oh," said Liz. "I think I'll just go as myself."